"I NEED A MILLION MORE STORIES ABOUT JORDYN AND MIKE...IT WAS SUPER FUN TO READ THIS NOVELLA. AND IT GAVE ME ALL THE FEELS. YOU'VE WRECKED ME FOR THE REST OF THE DAY."

ELLIE MALOUFF, AUTHOR OF THE LOVE OVERSEAS SERIES

"THIS IS TRULY ONE OF THE MOST JOYFUL BOOKS I'VE EVER READ! THERE'S BANTER, CHEMISTRY, LOVE OF ROMANCE NOVELS—AND I DARE YOU NOT TO SMILE THE ENTIRE TIME YOU'RE READING!"

SIERRA SIMONE, USA TODAY BESTSELLING AUTHOR

"IT GAVE THE KIND OF AMAZING HOPEFUL FEELINGS THAT I LOVE ABOUT ROMANCE NOVELS TO BEGIN WITH."

RILZY ADAMS, AUTHOR OF GO DEEP

"LUCY EDEN IS PARTICULARLY GOOD AT WRITING ROMANCES THAT MAKE MY HEART FEEL FULL AND THIS ONE IS NO DIFFERENT."

JODIE SLAUGHTER, AUTHOR OF ALL THINGS BURN & WHITE WHISKEY BARGAIN

"SO CUTE AND SWEET AND SEXY."

WILLOW ASTER, USA TODAY BESTSELLING AUTHOR

PRAISE FOR LUCY EDEN

EVERYTHING'S BETTER WITH YOU

"Everything's Better With You is a rare gem in the romance novel world. It has depth, great characters and a totally believable story line."

- The Laundry Librarian

EVERYTHING'S BETTER WITH KIMBERLY

"Engaging with attention to detail and kept me hooked from start to finish."

- Janine Caroline, Author of *I Look at You and Smile*

EVERYTHING'S BETTER WITH LISA

"Everything's Better with Lisa is refreshing, real and wonderfully entertaining. "

- Happily.Mary.After, Frolic Media

CHERISHING THE GODDESS

"The perfect balance of humor, angst, and steam. Highly recommended!"

- PE Kavanaugh, Author of *Sex, Money and the Price of Truth*

"This enemies to lovers romance will make your insides roar and you will want to pick up Lucy Eden's backlist immediately."

Cover Design & formatting: Lucy Eden

Editor: A.K Edits

Proofreader: Judy's Proofreading

Illustration: HellHoneyy

Every story is for my mom, who made me fall in love with reading & Ms. K, who made me fall in love with writing.

For Content Warnings (with spoilers) for all my books, please visit:

lucyeden.com/cw

————

Meet Jordyn, a 27yo programmer from NYC who came to Culver City, CA for the interview of a lifetime & Mike, the cute, funny & charming guy she meets in a bookstore.

Hi, I'm Jordyn. I flew from New York to Culver City, CA to interview for the job of a lifetime.

When I walked into The Bookstore, I only wanted a steamy romance or two to help pass the time before my big meeting.

I walked out with a gorgeous and sweet, cinnamon roll who was more funny and charming than all of my favorite book boyfriends combined, which definitely wasn't the plan.

But Mike was irresistible, and the time we spent together exploring Culver City was more fun than I've had in a long time.

But I'm smart enough to know if something feels to good too be true, it probably is.

I mean, Happily Ever Afters are just for fairy tales and romance novels ... right?

This standalone, blind date romance is full of swoony moments, cinnamon rolls, steam and has NO cheating.

*THE PAPERBACK EDITION INCLUDES THE ALL-NEW BONUS EPILOGUE: VEGAS, BABY!

BLIND DATE WITH A BOOK BOYFRIEND

A FUNNY DRAMATIC & STEAMY NOVELLA

LUCY EDEN

"HE WANTED A WIFE.

SHE WANTED TO GET PAID FOR MAKING A

WEDDING DRESS."

I FLIPPED THE BROWN PAPER–WRAPPED book over and tested its weight. Then flipped it over to read the label again. The words were printed on a HELLO MY NAME IS label.

The label on the display read "Blind Date with a Book" and was filled with wrapped books labeled with vague descriptions. The idea of any sort of blind date wasn't one that would normally appeal to me, but that was the old Jordyn Robbins. The new Jordyn Robbins got on an airplane by herself for a final interview at her dream job. The same dream job that would potentially take her away from her loving but overprotective parents and let her experience a type of freedom she wouldn't have in New York. The old Jordyn would never just buy a random book without knowing if she'd be spending the next five hours of her life with a duke, a billionaire, or bear shifter, but the new Jordyn—

"*The Duchess Deal,*" a deep voice called over my shoulder interrupting my train of thought.

"What?" I whipped around to face the person who I already knew was the most annoying person in the world, because no one comes to a bookstore to chat. Then I saw his face, and my mouth went dry. He was a tall, strikingly handsome guy who was smiling at me with stubbly dimpled cheeks, warm brown eyes, and a summer tan though it was winter. Was it winter here?

When I got on the plane at JFK, it was thirty-two degrees. When I got off the plane at LAX, it was seventy-nine. Do they have seasons here if it's in the seventies all year? These were things I would have to figure out if I was going to live here, but I was getting ahead of myself. I'd have to get through the interview first. I also realized that I'd been staring at Mr. Duchess Deal for an uncomfortably long time, and…yep, my mouth was open. I closed it and repeated myself.

"What?"

"The book you're holding." He jerked his chin at the brown paper packaging. "It's *The Duchess Deal* by Tessa Dare."

"Oh." I'd already read that one. I looked down at my hand, replaced the book on the shelf, and picked up another one.

"*The Princess Trap,*" he replied. I furrowed my brow at him and smiled.

"Who are you, the ghost of book boyfriends past?" I asked with a raised eyebrow. He responded with a deep chuckle that was contagious.

"No," he said in a sigh, followed by a smaller chuckle. "I'm just a guy who reads a lot of romance novels."

"Huh." I nodded suspiciously. My initial guess was that this man was buying a gift for a wife or girlfriend. Maybe I was being sexist. Why can't men read romance novels? They're good. But to be sure, I glanced at his left hand, no ring.

"Does that surprise you?"

"No," I lied. He raised a skeptical eyebrow. "Okay, a little. I've never met a guy who reads romance novels."

"Well, I'm honored to be your first." He grinned.

"Excuse me?" I glared at him. His smile dropped.

"No," he stammered. "I didn't mean that the way it came out. I'm sorry. I was trying to be charming, not creepy."

He reached up to tousle his messy dark brown hair, and his face flushed.

"Hi," a female voice called between us. We looked over to see one of the store's employees. She glared at the book whisperer before she turned to address me.

"Can I help you find something?" She gave me the pointed look that every woman knows is code for *Is this asshole bothering you, because I have a bat and a shovel?*

I smiled at Mr. Princess Trap, who somehow looked more embarrassed than he did before my would-be rescuer showed up.

"No, I'm fine. Thanks." I smiled at her.

She turned to him. "Can I help you find something?"

"No, I'm good. Thank you."

She walked towards the front of the store, straightening a stack of books on her way.

"Okay, that was awkward." His hand moved to the back of his neck and some of the color in his cheeks started to recede.

"What was awkward? Being asked if you needed help in a bookstore, or making virginity jokes with a stranger?" I raised an eyebrow.

"Um, both, but probably the second one...way more than the first."

I tucked my lips between my teeth to stifle a chuckle. He saw my reaction and smiled again.

"So, tell me about your first time," I said with a smirk. His smile faltered, and his shocked expression made me laugh again. "Reading a romance novel."

He narrowed his eyes at me, and his lips curled into a smile. "That's not fair. You get to make half-baked virginity jokes and I don't?"

"I don't make the rules." I shrugged.

"Well, my buddy's marriage was in trouble." He sighed and I felt my heart tug. "So a bunch of us guys started reading romance novels to help him win his wife back." That was incredibly sweet and somehow vaguely familiar, but I didn't know why. "He's a famous baseball player and he was away all the time—"

"Are you Kaiser Söze-ing me?"

"What? No?" He smiled.

"Really, because that's definitely the plot of *The Bromance Book Club*." I pointed to the Lyssa Kay Adams book on the shelf next to him.

"Fine." He raised his hands in surrender. "My older sister was obsessed with romance novels. So one day, I think she was sixteen and I was about twelve, I asked her what she was reading and she threw a shoe at me and told me to mind my own business, and naturally, I was curious. So, when she went out with her friends that night I snuck in her room and grabbed one." His face spread in a nostalgic grin. "I finished the whole thing in one night. I didn't sleep. Then I found out there were three more in the series and I spent the weekend reading those. Then, I spent the next two years sneaking romance novels out of her bedroom until she caught me. Then we started reading them together." He shrugged.

"That sounds adorable and not at all like the plot of a romance novel."

"It's true. I promise." He traced an X with his finger over the chest of his black t-shirt. "I'm Mike, by the way." He smiled at me with his eyebrows raised, waiting for a response.

"Jordyn," I responded.

"Well, Jordyn. You know all about my family. You've discovered one of my deepest, darkest secrets. Plus, you've seen my embarrassed face. And I know almost nothing about you, besides the fact that you also read romance novels and you must have the same odd sense of humor as I do or you would've walked away by now." He smiled again, and I snorted a laugh.

I began to weigh my options. I was in a strange city for a few days preparing for one of the most nerve-wracking experiences of my adult life. Maybe I could give in to Mike's terrible flirting. The plan was to buy a few books to take my mind off of the interview, but spending the last twenty minutes with a real live romance hero was doing the trick. What was the danger in a little harmless conversation?

"What do you want to know?" I asked.

"Do you come here often?"

"Wow," I chuckled. "You are really bad at flirting."

"Whoa. Slow down, Jordyn. Flirting? Really? You're coming on a little strong."

I laughed again. "Well, this is actually my first time here. It's actually my first time in California. I'm here for a few days for a work thing."

His eyes widened.

"Okay, I'm not gonna make a bad joke." He caught my skeptical expression, then added, "I'm not gonna make another bad joke, but if you're not busy, you should let me take you to lunch."

I tucked my bottom lip in between my teeth and bit down, trying to buy myself time. I tried to think. I've read enough romance novels to think that this was a great idea, but I've also listened to enough episodes of My Favorite Murder to think the exact opposite.

"I can tell you're on the fence, so why don't we let fate decide?"

"Okay, what do you have in mind?"

"You pick any one of these books." He gestured to the display of mystery books. "If I can guess which one it is, you'll let me take you to lunch...at a very public place."

I glanced at Mike for a few seconds before answering. I'm not sure why because I'd already made up my mind to say yes. My hesitation didn't come from the prospect of hanging out with a cute guy for a few hours. It was *this* cute guy with his terrible jokes, clumsy flirting, and maybe his dimples. My heart was beating out of my chest, and my belly was doing little fluttery things. It wasn't normal to feel this way about someone you just met.

Was it?

I was a grown woman who could spend a couple of hours with a friendly—and sexy—man and not make a big deal about it.

"Fine." I nodded, and he flashed me a grin. "But this isn't a date."

"Whoa, Jordyn. Slow down. Seriously." He held up his hands in defense and smirked.

I narrowed my eyes at him before scouring the display for the book with the vaguest explanation.

I held it up for inspection.

"Hmmm." Mike scratched his stubbled cheek, deep in thought.

2

"How did you know?"

Mike and I were walking down the sidewalk, and I was swinging the brown paper shopping bag full of books that I hoped I wouldn't have time to read before I left for New York.

"Come on… *Indigo*? That's a classic. Who hasn't read that book?" He laughed. "It was almost too easy." He shot me a suspicious look. "It's almost as if you wanted me to guess correctly so we could go on this *not a date* date."

"No, I was really trying to stump you. I obviously underestimated my opponent." That was mostly true. Secretly, I was hoping he would guess correctly. Mike sparked something in me. Was it curiosity or the same longing for change that drew me to California in the first place? Whatever it was I wanted to follow where it led. I looked up at him and he smiled. My stomach did a flip that could have been attributed to hunger, but I suspected it wasn't.

"Well, sometimes being underestimated is a good thing." He laughed and reached for my shopping bag. "Hey, let me carry those."

"No." I held the bag out of his reach, shivering at his touch when his fingertips brushed the back of my hand. "You insisted on paying for them. At least let me carry them."

"Fine."

We walked along the tree-lined street in silence, letting the warm breeze caress our faces. The silence wasn't awkward but comfortable. I still hadn't told Mike anything about myself, but I wanted to. I also felt safe with him. I could only imagine what my parents would say if I told them I met a strange guy in a bookstore and left with him. I wonder if this is how it feels when you meet the person you will eventually fall in love with, or when you meet the person who is about to murder you. I imagined the salesperson telling the police, "I knew something was off with that dude, but she left with him anyway. Tragic!" She tried to rescue me, but I was led out of the store and to my death by dimples.

"Hey." Mike's voice interrupted my chain of thought. "You okay?"

"Yeah," I laughed, "why?"

"You seemed a little out of it for a second."

"What? No. Just got stuck daydreaming."

"Oh, yeah?" He smiled, and his deadly dimples returned. "What were you daydreaming about?"

"Nothing." I tried for an innocent smile.

"Come on, tell me. You're still a complete mystery, Jordyn. I'm feeling a little exposed."

We stopped at an intersection of a busy road, waiting for the light to change. I turned to face him.

"I was wondering if you were a serial killer," I blurted out and raised my eyebrows to look up at him. His eyes went wide, and he barked out a laugh. He definitely wasn't expecting me to say that.

"Wow. Okay." He laughed. "I'm not a serial killer, but if I was, I probably wouldn't tell you... Wait, how many people would I need to have killed to make me a serial killer?"

"Three," I replied with a giggle.

"Okay, then I'm definitely not a serial killer." He put his hand on his chest in mock relief and I rolled my eyes, trying to suppress a laugh.

"You're a goofball."

"Is that a good thing?" he asked.

"So far." I smiled. "We'll see how lunch goes."

"For what it's worth, I've never killed anyone. I did punch a guy for bullying my sister."

"I thought your sister was older."

"I have two sisters. One older, one younger."

I nodded.

"Hey, that's something else you know about me. Not fair. I'm a vault until you start talking."

I eyed him for a moment before speaking. "So... where are you taking me for lunch?" I smirked at him.

He narrowed his eyes at me and smiled.

"I can be patient."

The light changed, and Mike grabbed my hand as we stepped off of the curb.

"Is this okay, Jordyn?" He glanced at our interlocked hands, then into my eyes, and for a moment, my heart stopped beating, and I couldn't speak for a few seconds.

"Yeah, yes. It's fine." I gave his hand a reassuring squeeze. "But I haven't held hands while crossing the street in a while."

"Old habits die hard."

————

MIKE LED me to a restaurant called Public School 310. It was a pub-style restaurant that had a school lunch theme. He pulled out a stool for me to sit on before seating himself.

"This place is cute." I picked up the menu. It was designed like a composition book. "I don't remember being able to get Maker's Mark with my tater tots in the second grade."

"Really? My school had gin martinis on pizza day."

I narrowed my eyes at him and smirked.

"So, does the food taste like cafeteria food?"

"I wouldn't bring a woman I'm trying to impress to a place that didn't have amazing food."

I froze at his words and glanced up at him but he was scouring the menu, completely ignoring the fact that he just told me he was trying to impress me.

So corny, but why was it working?

"So, is this like your date spot?" I tried to remember that I'd only known Mike for a couple of hours, and he probably trolled romance bookstores looking for single women. "Do you bring a lot of women here?"

"No, this is one of my favorite places to eat in the city." He closed the menu, crossed his arms over his chest, and leaned forward. "And this isn't a date, remember?"

"Right."

Because who agrees to go on a date with someone they met less than an hour ago?

"Hey, Mike." Our server came to the table and dropped off two glasses of water. She was tall and thin, with long curly red hair pulled into a ponytail.

"Hey, Linds." He smiled at her before turning his attention to me. "This is Jordyn. She's from New York, and this is her first time in Culver City."

"Cool. Nice to meet you. I'm Lindsay, I'll be your server, and you have the perfect guide to show you around."

"So, he comes here a lot?" I asked Lindsay, and I noticed Mike lean forward and narrow his eyes at me.

"Oh, yeah. Mike is definitely a regular." She nodded sagely.

"Does he come in here with a lot of different women?" I'd asked the question to tease Mike, but I wasn't completely sure I was ready for the answer.

Mike was mid-sip of water and I heard him snort before descending into a coughing fit.

"No, not for a long time. Mike is definitely one of the good ones." She smiled at the man sitting across from me who was not my date, but I was kinda wishing he was. "And he's a very generous tipper. Like, extremely generous."

I caught Mike's eye, and we shared a laugh.

"So, are you ready to order?" Lindsay held up a small notepad.

"I am. Jordyn?"

"Yeah. I'm gonna have a tequila mockingbird…um, oh, the bacon cheddar tots…and the steak, medium, with a side of Brussel sprouts."

"Great. Mike?"

"I'll get the Valkyrie on tap and the burger."

Lindsay scooped up our menus and walked away.

"That was sneaky." He let out a small residual cough and took another sip of water.

I shrugged and tried for another innocent smile.

"So, if this isn't a date, why would you care if I brought other women here?"

I opened my mouth to answer, then I closed it because I didn't have a good answer. I felt like I was free-falling. Mike was cute, funny, and charming. I wanted to know more about him. I wanted him to know more about me. Also, I wondered what it might be like to kiss him and—

Shit. I think we're on a date.

"Is it weird that this feels like a date?" I asked.

"No, because I'm pretty sure this turned into a date when you started flirting with me in the bookstore."

I burst out laughing.

"I think you're confusing a few key details."

"I don't think so." He took another sip of water.

"So, you don't go to that bookstore to pick up women."

"No." He laughed. "That was my first time there."

"But you live in the neighborhood and you love romance novels. How is that possible?"

"Well…" He shifted uncomfortably in his chair. "You already know, my sister also loved romance novels. We ordered most of them online and there are limited selections in bookstores, but we'd always get those weird judgmental looks."

"Yes, I'm familiar with the side-eye."

"We always used to talk about what it would be like to have a bookstore that only sold romance. She would've loved that place."

"Loved?"

"Yeah." He sighed. "She died five years ago. Car accident. Some asshole on his phone."

"I'm so sorry."

"Yeah, me too. So, I've always been meaning to go in, but it always made me think of her. But for some reason, I just decided that today was the day."

Lindsay dropped off our drinks.

"Sorry, that was probably a mood killer." He pulled his beer closer to himself and began slowly turning the glass on the table and didn't meet my eye.

"No, it wasn't. Thank you for sharing that with me, and I'm glad you came into the store today."

"You are?" His face snapped up to meet mine.

"Yeah. I mean, I was planning on hanging out in my Airbnb all weekend, reading books and ordering DoorDash. But instead, I'm here with you, getting ready to day drink and eat tater tots for the first time in over a decade." My face was burning, and this moment felt oddly vulnerable, but I managed to smile at him, glad he wouldn't be able to tell I was blushing.

"Wait, you flew all the way to sunny California from New York in the middle of winter to sit in an Airbnb all weekend?"

"That's technically not the purpose of my trip, but that was definitely plan A."

"Well, plan B is you spend the rest of the day with me, and I'll show you all the cool stuff in Culver City."

"Cooler than a romance bookstore and a school cafeteria with a full bar?"

"Absolutely. But in exchange, you have to talk about yourself."

"Why?" I laughed.

"Because I don't know how you managed to do it, but in the past three hours, I've revealed more personal things about myself than I think I have in years, and I barely know anything about you. Now, I'm feeling more than a little exposed."

I laughed again and held out my hand across the table. Mike engulfed my small hand with his, and I felt the familiar stomach-swooping and heart-racing feelings I'd felt when he held my hand in the street. We shook hands.

"Deal," I said, and Mike answered me with a grin. "Should we toast?" I held up my drink.

"Sure. What should we toast to?"

"What's your sister's name?"

His eyes met mine, his smile faltered, and he paused. For a split second, I was nervous that I'd done the wrong thing by bringing her up again.

"Lola… Well, her name is, was, Laura. I'm the only one that called her Lola because I couldn't pronounce her name when I was learning to talk and she never corrected me." He let out a small nostalgic chuckle while continuing to stare into his beer. My eyes stung a little and I got the sense that Mike didn't talk about his sister often.

"To Laura?" I asked. He looked up from his drink and met my eye. His expression was confusing. It was like a mix of gratitude and adoration with a tinge of sadness.

"To Laura," he whispered and held up his pint.

We nodded and we clinked glasses.

3

"OKAY, so if you were on a date with a woman and you wanted to convince her that you weren't a serial killer, this is the last place you should bring her."

Mike laughed as he held the door open to The Museum of Jurassic Technology. The outside was small and unassuming, but after peering inside, I was greeted with a dark hall with hauntingly illuminated displays. It looked like a place Tim Burton would go to cheer himself up. I raised a skeptical eyebrow at Mike.

"You're gonna love this place, trust me, and there are plenty of witnesses." He did have a point. There were plenty of people around, and he hadn't steered me wrong so far.

I kept my skeptical expression as I passed under the arm that was holding the door open and walked inside.

"So, what exactly is Jurassic Technology?" I asked as we passed a display that held a pair of old dice.

"I'll be honest with you. I have no idea, but this is a creepy museum full of cool shit…and there's free tea and cookies."

"Free tea and cookies? You definitely should've led with that."

We walked around the weirdest museum I'd ever seen, and I continued to answer Mike's questions.

I told him that I'd grown up in Harlem and Brooklyn. I was an only child, and my parents were doctors. I'd graduated from MIT with a BS in computer science and engineering. I'd spent the last four years working at different start-ups and was looking for something more stable. He changed the subject to romance novels, which didn't surprise me. Usually, when I started talking about programming, people's eyes started to glaze over with boredom.

"Well, my mother and her sister are addicts. They even go on an annual cruise hosted by their favorite romance author. But, I have to admit that even though I had a lot of access to *the good stuff*—my mom and aunt's words—I also side-eyed them until my freshman year in college."

Mike gasped in feigned indignation and shook his head at me. I huffed out a small chuckle.

"My brain was fried from finals, and I wanted to read something that wasn't Mathematical Structures or Computer Simulations, so while I was home on break, I picked up one of my mom's books. And well, I quickly realized how wrong I was about romance novels, and now I'm hooked." I shrugged.

"Well, at least you realized the error of your ways when you were still young."

"Ha ha," I deadpanned. "Hey, are those dead mice on a piece of bread?" I scowled at another display case.

Mike turned his head to look at the exhibit I was pointing to.

"Yup. It appears so… Hey, you ready for those free cookies? I think the tea room is closing soon."

"Looking at dead mice on a piece of bread made you want cookies?"

"Free cookies, Jordyn. I never say no to free cookies."

I laughed as Mike slipped my hand into his and led me to the tea room.

————

"Okay, your dad's a neurosurgeon and your mom's a pediatric oncologist?"

I nodded. Mike's plan to impress me was working so far. It was as if he'd memorized everything I'd told him about myself.

"And they met in med school?"

"Yes, they were two of the few Black med students at Columbia, so they ended up running in the same circle of friends…and they ended up together."

"That's cool. And then they had you."

"Yup. It's funny because they initially didn't want kids. One day, my mom asked the mother of one of her patients if she knew about her daughter's diagnosis before she had her and what was in store, would she still have gone through with it. The woman said that there's never a way to predict a favorable outcome. There's never a right time, a perfect amount of money, or an instruction manual. There's only love and everything in life is an unpredictable leap of faith." I shrugged.

"So, my mom talked to my dad and they decided to try for a baby before learning it wasn't as easy as they thought it would be. Four years and three rounds of IVF later, I was born." I shrugged again and took a bite of my cookie. "That felt like TMI. Was that TMI... Sorry." I accidentally sprayed Mike with crumbs.

"No, not at all." He was giving me the most adorable smile, and it made my chest feel warm, but maybe that was the residual effects of the tequila I had at lunch. "That's actually a much nicer story than how my parents met."

"Really? Spill." I brought my teacup to my lips.

"Well, my dad won my mom in a poker game. A week later, they got married, and my sister was born nine months later."

"What?" I spluttered, almost choking on my tea. Mike shrugged and took an exaggerated sip from his teacup, pinky out and everything. "Um, no. There has to be more to that story. Please, tell me there's more to that story."

He gave me a coy smile before taking a deep breath, evidently having tortured me enough.

"So, my mom is a former model and pageant queen. When she was Miss Colombia, she participated in a charity casino night at the Beverly Hills Hotel. There was a poker tournament, and the prize was dinner with my mom." He laughed at my expression of mild outrage. "It's not what you're thinking. It was a photo op. They sat at a table in one of the hotel's restaurants. Mom wore her crown and sash while she and Dad posed for pictures. Totally innocent and staged, but Dad charmed my mom that night and they were inseparable after that."

"Okay, that's actually really sweet. You definitely need to work on the way you tell that story."

Mike smiled and looked at his watch.

"Last call for cookies?" he said before putting his hands on his knees and pushing himself up to stand.

"I think I'm good on cookies."

"Cool. We have another hour before the museum closes. Wanna walk around some more?"

"As long as we can avoid the dead mice on bread."

"We definitely can, but I can't guarantee you won't see something worse."

I laughed as Mike helped me to my feet. I hooked my arm around his bicep. "Is this okay?" I asked.

"Yeah. It's perfect." He covered the hand that was holding his bicep with one of his own. "So, what happened to the lady's kid? Your mom's patient?"

"Oh, she's been cancer-free for over thirty years. Our families still keep in touch, and I'm named after her."

4

WHEN WE FINALLY LEFT THE museum, the sun was beginning to set.

"So, what now?"

"You still want to hang out? I don't want you getting tired of me." He squeezed my hand.

"Well, you're not in danger of that yet, but the night is still young."

We were walking past a statue of a lion standing on its hind legs with its arms outstretched, wearing a robe in the middle of alternating jets of water that sprayed from the sidewalk.

"What's the story there?" I pointed.

"That's the lion's fountain."

"The lion's fountain?" I furrowed my eyebrows.

"Yeah...?"

"I mean, Culver City is home to some of the best storytellers in the world and this is the best name they could come up with?"

Mike barked out another laugh.

"Okay, brainiac, what would you name it?"

"I don't know, but something better. Like, why is it wearing a robe? Is it dancing? Why is it standing on two legs? What's the significance of the water? Where does a lion get a robe? Who made—"

My barrage of questions was interrupted by Mike pressing his lips to mine. His large palms glided over my cheeks, holding me in place for him as his warm breath caressed my face. My heart was pounding out of my chest and my skin was shimmering with electricity. I started to reach my arms up to wrap around his neck and part my lips to deepen our kiss when he pulled away quickly with a loud smacking sound... too quickly.

"Shit. I'm sorry. I shouldn't have done that...just kissed you like that." He reached up to grab the back of his neck. His face was red like it had been in the bookstore, and I was still recovering from his unexpected, yet very welcome, kiss. It couldn't have lasted more than a few seconds, but it stole my breath and was overwhelming in the best way. I'd never been kissed like that before. Mike had kissed me like it was the most important thing he would ever do in his life. And while I understood and appreciated why he stopped himself, I wanted more.

"Hey. It's okay," I said, still feeling the ghost of his lips on mine.

"No, it wasn't. It was spending all this time with you... And you're so beautiful and smart and funny. Then the sunset was so perfect." He gestured at the darkening sky. "And you were asking all those questions about the fountain, and it was so fucking hilarious and cute..."

I tucked my lips between my teeth to keep from laughing at him when he was clearly doing way too much.

"Did I fuck this up?" He raised his eyebrows in question.

"No." And I couldn't hold back a chuckle. "You didn't fuck this up."

"Good," he said in a sigh. He looked genuinely relieved, and it was kind of endearing. "So, did you come up with a name yet?"

"No, I was a little distracted." I smiled at him. His cheeks were still pink. "Too soon?" I smirked.

I walked over to where he was and stood next to him, facing the fountain, and put my head on his shoulder. He wrapped his arm around my waist and squeezed. We watched the water in the fountain dance in rhythm around the lion for a while before a group of kids ran into the jets, squealing and splashing each other.

"That looks like fun," I said.

"Wanna try it?" He squeezed my hip again.

"No." I cut my eyes at his absurd suggestion.

"Why not?"

"Okay, first of all, it's a terrible idea. And second of all, I can't get my hair wet."

"Why can't you get your hair wet?" He reached up and twirled a lock of my hair around his finger before releasing it. Usually, unsolicited hair-touching wasn't something I'd tolerate, but for some reason I didn't mind when Mike did it.

Shit. I liked him.

"Because I went to the salon and got it done for my very important work thing on Monday, and I need to make it last until then."

"Fair enough." He nodded and returned his hand to my hip.

"But you should go."

"Not without you."

"Come on. I dare you."

"Okay." He turned to face me before putting his hands on my hips and turning me to face him. "If I run through that fountain, I want something in return."

"What?" I asked, biting my lip, hoping the answer was another kiss.

"I want another kiss." His smile faded, and I suddenly felt like I was in the middle of a serious business negotiation. Mike could've had all the kisses he wanted without running through the fountain, but that didn't mean I couldn't have a little fun.

"Fine"—I held out my hand for another shake—"but you have to really get in there, not a quick jump in and jump out."

"Whatever the lady wants." Mike began to toe off his sneakers and unbutton his pants.

"What are you doing?" I squealed.

"I'm not gonna run through there with my clothes on." He continued to undress to whoops and hollers from the gathering crowd. I turned around to see that Mike had more than a few admirers, female and otherwise. I could see why.

He was standing in front of me in a white tank top and black boxer briefs. Every muscle on his six-foot-something frame was chiseled, well-defined, and incredibly distracting, and not just to me.

"See something you like?" Mike's mocking tone alerted me to the fact that my eyes had traveled further south than I intended, and I felt my face heat.

"Shut up and get in the fountain, pretty boy," I said.

"Yeah, get in the fountain!" a high-pitched female voice squealed beside me. She was a tall, thin, pretty girl who looked a couple of years younger than me, with waist-length brown hair and a deep tan, wearing knee-high Uggs, denim cut-off shorts, and an off-the-shoulder sweatshirt with the strings of a pink bikini tied around her neck. Before I could think twice about it, I reached up, grabbed the back of Mike's neck and pulled him down for a kiss. The crowd cheered.

"What was that?" he asked with a grin when our lips separated.

"A down payment," I whispered.

It definitely wasn't jealousy or some weird primal urge to claim Mike as mine, because that wouldn't make any sense. Would it?

"You know this is a double standard, right?"

"I don't make the rules."

"I'm not complaining," he laughed.

"Give me your phone. We should memorialize this."

Mike reached into the pile of clothes I was holding in my arms, retrieved his phone, unlocked it, and then handed it to me.

"Go!" I said, holding up the phone.

Mike took off running toward the fountain and almost slipped on the slick stone surface, making the crowd gasp. Once he secured his footing, he raised his fists in triumph and the crowd cheered. He then began strutting through the jets of water like Mick Jagger while the crowd clapped a beat, succeeding in getting himself soaking wet. Mike's water show continued with more silly dance moves, during which he was joined by more kids, and I was laughing so hard I couldn't hold the phone straight. He finished his routine with a poorly executed moonwalk before he held out his hands with his eyebrows raised in question and yelled, "Are you not entertained?!"

I nodded, still laughing, and he walked toward me with his deadly dimples on full display. The white tank top clung to his chest and torso, outlining well-defined pecs and what was definitely a washboard.

"That was amazing," a voice called from beside me. It was the woman in the Ugg boots, and she was joined by a slightly older man who had his arm around her waist. She was holding a towel. "Here. We just drove in from the beach and we always carry spares."

"Thanks." Mike grabbed the towel and started drying off.

"Babe," she addressed the man holding her. "This guy jumped into the fountain to impress this pretty girl. Remind you of anyone?" She planted a kiss on his lips, and I noticed her giant diamond ring.

"I would dive into a million fountains for you, baby doll."

"I'm Cam, and this is Beckett." She tilted her head at her husband. "We've been together for twenty years," she said proudly.

Twenty years?!

This woman would have to be at least in her late thirties. How was that possible? "Married for fifteen. How about you two?"

I was too stunned to speak. Then I realized that I'd have to tell this woman that I'd only met Mike this morning. Before I could open my mouth, Mike put his hand on my shoulder and spoke for the both of us.

"Three years." He winked at me when I shot him a questioning glance.

"That's so cool. You thinking about getting married?" she asked as Mike handed her the damp towel, thanking her.

"Yeah, I keep asking and she keeps turning me down." He sighed and shook his head. I narrowed my eyes at him.

"I'm holding out for a ring like yours," I replied to our nosy new friend, and I heard Mike snort a laugh under his breath.

"You're smart." She tapped her forehead sagely. "But don't keep him on the hook too long. There are only a few good ones left."

"I'll keep that in mind." I smiled at her, and Mike and I watched her lock hands with her husband and walk away.

"Okay." I whipped around to face him. "How old do you think that woman was?"

"I don't know," Mike shrugged. "Twenty-four. Fifty-seven. It's hard to tell sometimes. And I wasn't really paying attention to her." He gazed down at me before using the back of his fingertips to caress my face. His fingers were still damp with a slight chill, and it was oddly refreshing.

"Do you have a hair tie?"

"Do… Do you need a hair tie?"

Mike laughed at my confused expression.

"Don't all women walk around with a hair tie on their wrist?"

"No. Not all women."

He reached under the pile of clothes I was carrying, grabbed my wrist and held it up. There was a thin black hair elastic under my watchband.

"That's anecdotal, and it proves nothing," I said.

"I'm gonna get dressed, and you're gonna use that hair tie to put your hair up, because I'm about to kiss the hell out of you and I don't want to be responsible for any collateral damage."

5

AND KISS the hell out of me, he did. After he got dressed and I pulled my hair up into a messy top knot, Mike wrapped one arm around my waist and wrapped his other hand around the back of my neck and pulled me into him.

"Fuck, you're beautiful," he whispered before he closed the distance between our mouths. I didn't waste any time before wrapping my arms around his neck and parting my lips, sliding my tongue into his eager mouth. He let out a low growl when I pressed myself onto my tiptoes and clutched handfuls of his wet hair. I didn't want him to have any doubt that this was exactly what I wanted. Every inch of my flesh was shimmering with electricity. Mike's palm roamed my back and his fingertips grazed the skin along the waistband of my jeans, radiating heat to the rest of my body.

If we were in a movie, it would be one of those shots where they put the camera on one of those circular train-track thingies, a song like "Kiss Me" by Sixpence None The Richer would play, and digital fireflies would be added in post-production. If the crowd's reaction was any indication, "Pony" by Ginuwine would have been a more accurate song choice. A chorus of howls and whistles surrounded us with cries of "Get a room, you two," and someone definitely said, "They are gonna fuuuuuck," making us laugh so hard that we broke our kiss.

"We should stop," I whispered.

"You're probably right," he said before brushing his lips over mine again. I giggled.

"So, where are you taking me now?" I asked, pressing two fingers over my lips, which were tingling with sensation.

"Wow. I definitely did not plan this far ahead. I was sure I would have driven you off by now." He began to look around before he paused and pointed behind him. "Movie?"

I liked the idea of spending time in a dark enclosed space with Mike, so I nodded. We walked to the ArcLight and bought two tickets for the next movie.

By some stroke of divine intervention, I got to spend two hours looking at Chris Evans and kissing Mike's face off in a dark corner of the theater. I even let him get to second base.

"Were you thinking about Chris Evans when you were kissing me?" Mike asked with a smirk when we left the theater, hand in hand.

"Do you want me to say no, or tell you the truth?" I tucked my bottom lip between my teeth and grinned up at him. Mike answered me with a deep belly laugh before leaning down and planting a kiss on my lips. "Would it make you feel better if I told you that I was thinking about you and Chris Evans at the same time?"

Mike paused mid-step and furrowed his brow in mock concentration for a second before nodding. "Actually, yeah. That does make me feel better."

I laughed and playfully slapped him on the chest. He covered my hand with his, and we continued to walk.

"So, what did you think about the movie?" he asked.

"I thought it was great."

"What was your favorite part?"

"Hmm." I had to think because I honestly didn't remember watching the movie. "The part where they took the knives out?" I smiled innocently at him and shrugged.

Mike snorted a laugh and said, "I love you."

My heart stopped and I looked up at him. "What?"

"I meant I love your sense of humor. You're so funny." Mike blushed again.

"Mm-hmm." I gave him a skeptical look.

"Seriously."

"Well, I love the way your face turns red when you're embarrassed."

Mike flushed brighter and wiped a hand over his face.

"Thank my dad for that."

"Thanks, Mike's dad." I grinned at him, and he kissed me before we stopped in front of another building.

"I want to take you one more place before we call it a night."

"Mike." I looked up at a brightly lit canopy and people walking in and out with luggage. "This is a hotel." I narrowed my eyes at him.

"Really, Jordyn? After everything we've been through?" He hit me with a mock scandalized expression. "Get your mind out of the gutter."

I laughed again as he led me inside, but I'm pretty sure my mind had been in the gutter since he kissed me.

We ended up in a bar on the second floor. Mike ordered himself a Voodoo IPA and I decided to stick with tequila and ordered a cocktail called The Wicked Witch.

"This place is pretty cool." I nodded, looking around.

"Told you." He smirked. "So, what should we toast to this time?"

"Hmm." I tapped my chin. "To Montague."

"Montague?"

"That's what I named the lion. His friends call him Monty."

Mike laughed again. "Okay, to Monty."

"To Monty."

We clinked our glasses together and took a sip. My drink was spicier than I was expecting, and it made my lips pucker.

"Good?" he asked.

"Very good," I responded, and noticed he had a thin mustache of foam on his upper lip. I reached out and wiped it away with the pad of my thumb. Mike captured my wrist and sucked the tip of my thumb into his mouth.

"Mike," I whisper-shouted. "We're in public."

"I don't care." He leaned forward and kissed me.

"Well, I do," I laughed and pushed him away.

"Fine"—he fake-pouted—"but this isn't over."

I chuckled and looked around the bar. It was dark and sexy with a lot of wood and red velvet.

"This lounge is designed to look like a prohibition-style speakeasy."

"That's cool." I reached for my glass.

"And when the Wizard of Oz was being filmed, the actors that played the munchkins threw wild parties, had orgies, and trashed the hotel."

I froze with my drink halfway to my mouth.

"For real?"

"Allegedly." He shrugged and took another sip of his beer.

"So, you brought me to a speakeasy in a hotel famous for its orgies?"

"When you put it that way, I guess I did." He chuckled.

"I approve." I nodded and took another sip of my drink. I snuggled next to Mike on the velvet couch, and he put his arm around my shoulder.

"So, your mom is Colombian?"

"Born and raised."

"And your dad?"

"Dad was born and raised in Chicago and he is Irish, Scottish, and Italian."

"What do your parents do?"

"Well, my dad is a semi-retired entertainment lawyer and my mom ran a modeling school for a while, but now she does pageant consulting."

"Did your sisters ever model?"

"My mom forbade them from ever going into modeling so, of course, my little sister, Erica, has been modeling since she was sixteen."

"How old is she now?"

"Twenty-three."

"How old are you?"

"Thirty."

"Do you speak Spanish?"

"A little. The only person I ever spoke Spanish with regularly was my grandmother, and after she passed away"—he shrugged—"I guess I got out of practice. It's a little embarrassing."

"Your grandmother lived in the US?" I asked.

"My grandmother lived with us. When my parents got married and Mom found out she was pregnant, my grandmother moved in to help out and stayed." He shrugged again.

"That must have been nice."

"Yeah, it was. She had the best laugh, and she loved practical jokes. She was also lethal with a wooden spoon. Watching her and my dad fight was always hilarious."

"Really?"

"Yes, my grandmother refused to learn English, and Dad never learned to speak Spanish aside from a couple of words, but that wouldn't stop them from having all-day screaming matches. Sometimes, Mom would translate, but usually, she would ignore them." He laughed at the memory, and I found something else I loved about him.

"That must have been tough for them."

Mike laughed. "Nah. Those two loved each other. It was the weirdest thing. My dad lost his mom when he was a kid, so I think my grandmother was like the mother he never had. Her funeral was the first time I'd ever seen him cry... Hey, what's wrong?"

"Nothing." I wiped my eyes. "It's the tequila. That's the sweetest thing I've ever heard."

"Well, I can't end the night with you in tears." He planted a kiss on the top of my head and sat up. "Do you want another one?"

I nodded.

"Same thing, or something different?"

"Surprise me."

Mike signaled for a server, ordered himself another beer, and a drink for me called Glinda the Good Witch. "To balance things out," he said.

"I have another question for you."

"Another question?" Mike laughed.

"Yes. Am I asking too many questions?" The drinks were making me sentimental, giddy, and a little bold.

"Never. Ask away."

"Do you consider yourself an alpha, beta, cinnamon roll, alphahole or rake?"

"Hmm, I never thought about it? I did go through a rake phase in college." He shrugged. "What do you think I am?"

"Wait, go back to your rake phase."

"Ugh. I'm not proud of it, but I was a horny college kid who'd spent most of my teenage years reading books that contained a lot of different ways to seduce and satisfy women."

"You used your powers for evil." I gasped and slapped him on the bicep.

"I wouldn't go that far." He bopped my nose with his fingertip. "Now, answer my question."

"I wasn't sure at first, but after you freaked out about that kiss at the fountain... definitely a cinnamon roll." I tried to stifle a laugh.

"I didn't freak out."

"You kinda did, but I thought it was sweet." I leaned up and kissed him.

"Hmph," he snorted.

"Why did you tell Cam that we'd been together for three years?"

"Mostly because I didn't want to tell her that I stripped down to my underwear and jumped in a fountain for a girl I'd only met eight hours ago."

"Are you ashamed that you made a fool of yourself publicly for a kiss?"

"I would dive into a million fountains for you, baby doll." Mike mimicked Beckett's voice and I giggled for longer than I'd meant to, making him chuckle. "And partly because I wish I'd met you three years ago." He kissed me again. "I have a question for you," he asked when our lips separated.

"We have been together for three years, so…" I shrugged. "What do you want to know?"

"What's your super important work thing on Monday?"

"It's a job interview."

"Okay…" He raised his eyebrows, apparently not satisfied with that answer.

"I'm sorry if it seems like I'm being cryptic. It's not like a top secret, CIA-type interview. I'm just really excited about it, and I'm afraid if I talk about it too much, I'll jinx it. I know it's silly."

"It's not silly."

Mike had spent this entire day opening himself up to me and sharing his innermost secrets. It felt weird keeping this one bit of information from him.

"It is." I sighed and continued, "I'll just tell you. You've told me practically everything there is to know about you. The least I can do is tell you about my interview at Grayson Technology."

I felt Mike's muscles twitch in the arm that was draped around my shoulder.

"Did you say Grayson Technology?"

"Yeah, have you heard of it? I mean I guess you would have, you're like the mayor of Culver City." I laughed, and I noticed that Mike went pale—well, paler.

"Are you okay?"

"Yeah, I'm fine. It's getting late. I should take you home." He sat up, forcing me to sit up too, before rising to his feet.

"Are you sure you're okay? You looked a little out of it for a second. Where'd you go?"

"I'm fine. I was wondering if you were a serial killer." He winked at me before pulling me to my feet and leading me out of the hotel.

6

"WHY ARE WE IN AN UBER? We can walk to my Airbnb." Mike helped me into a black SUV, buckled my seatbelt, and climbed in beside me.

"We're going to grab some food. You haven't had anything to eat since lunch except for movie popcorn and Reese's Pieces."

"I had cookies at the museum," I pointed out, with a sleepy giggle.

"You need food." Mike wrapped his arm around my shoulder and used the pad of this thumb to caress the back of my neck.

With my head on his shoulder, I closed my eyes. Mike pressed a gentle kiss on the top of my head before softly whispering the word "shit."

I wanted to ask him about it, but the day caught up with me and my eyelids got heavy.

———

I WOKE up to the sound of a car door closing and Mike sliding into the back seat next to me carrying two bags of food. My stomach rumbled loudly in response to the smell of grilled meat and fried potatoes.

"Was that your stomach?" he asked.

"I guess I am a little hungry," I giggled.

"Then I guess I better feed you." He kissed me again. "Where are you staying?"

I gave him the address before resting my head on his shoulder again and drifting off.

———

WE STOOD outside the door of the apartment I'd rented while I fumbled with the keys. I finally got the door open, walked inside, toed off my sneakers, and tossed my purse and the shopping bag of books on the kitchen table. Mike stood outside the apartment, holding the bags. He looked unsure of whether or not he should come in.

"What are you doing?" I laughed. "Get in here."

"I don't know if that's a good idea, Jordyn."

I crossed to the door, grabbed his wrist with both hands, and pulled him inside.

"You are not going to make me eat by myself." I set the bags down on the table and started to unpack them. "This smells amazing. I've heard good things about In-N-Out Burger." I smiled and waggled my eyebrows as Mike dropped into one of the chairs. "Okay, what am I eating here?"

"That is a double-double, animal style"—he pointed at a giant greasy burger with two patties and loaded with toppings—"with fries, also animal style." There was a container of fries loaded with the same toppings as the burger.

"What is animal style?" I slid one of the fries out of the container and popped it in my mouth. Whatever it was, it was good.

"Animal style means you want your food with melted cheese, secret sauce, and fried onions. It's my go-to hangover prevention."

"Mike, are you drunk?" I flopped into his lap and wrapped my arms around his neck.

"I'm not," he said in a chuckle, "but I know someone who is."

"I don't know what you're talking about. I'm not drunk, I'm nice."

"What does nice mean?"

"Nice means I'm sober enough to consent to a sexual encounter but tipsy enough that I don't care that I'm wearing giant gray cotton underwear that may or may not have a hole in them."

Mike rested his forehead on my shoulder, and I could feel his chest shaking with laughter.

"Oh my God, Jordyn." He planted a kiss on the back of my neck. "Eat first, then we'll talk about your giant underwear later."

We ate our late-night carb, meat, and cheese feast as I continued to sit on Mike's lap.

"I think this is the best food I've ever had," I said through a mouth full of burger.

"I think that's the tequila talking."

"Tequila is very smart." I finished my milkshake with a slurp. "So, what now?"

"Now, you go to bed and I go home."

"Boo." I stood and began to clear the table, tossing the empty food wrappers and containers in the kitchen trash. "What's with you? I thought we were having a good time."

"We're having a great time."

"So, don't go home right away…unless you have to get up early in the morning, or you are actually getting tired of this." I made a circular gesture around my face with my index finger. I hoped I was making a joke, but I was nervous that I wasn't.

"Not possible." Mike grabbed a cloth from the kitchen counter and wiped down the table. Afterwards, we sat on the couch and talked about the highlights of the last twelve hours.

"Did your parents really get married after only a week?" I said in a loud yawn.

"Yes, Sleeping Beauty, they did," Mike said in a chuckle.

"That's a little unconventional. Isn't it?"

"Well, conventional is definitely not a word I would use to describe my parents, but they both said that it couldn't have happened any other way. They met and they knew... Jordyn?"

"Hmm?" I was vaguely aware that my eyes were closed.

"You're falling asleep."

"No, I'm not."

"Your eyes are closed."

"I'm just resting them."

Mike chuckled, stood from the couch, lifted me in his arms, and carried me to the bedroom. He set me down on the mattress and covered me with the duvet. I felt him press a kiss to my forehead as he knelt by the bed.

"Are you really leaving?" Spending the day with him had been the most fun I'd had in a long time and I wasn't ready for it to end.

"I think it's best."

"Well, I disagree. I'm pretty sure I'm not drunk anymore, but I am really tired."

"So I'll let you sleep."

"Would you sleep with me… I mean, just sleep," I giggled. "I would definitely be down for other stuff, but I'm pretty exhausted, and I don't know how good I would be."

Mike laughed again before crawling into bed behind me and wrapping his arms around my waist.

"Did you take your shoes off?" I asked.

"Of course."

"I have to get up." I moved his arm and sat up to face him. "Look, I have to wash my face, put on night cream, and I have to wrap my hair in a scarf. It's not the cutest look, but it's necessary."

"Okay." Mike shrugged.

"Okay?" I asked and narrowed my eyes.

"I grew up with four women and they all slept in silk turbans. The only times I'd ever seen my mom without makeup was when she was wearing a face mask."

"Really?"

"Yeah, I thought all women slept in them until I started dating." Mike shrugged and I let out a tequila-fueled giggle while imagining him asking the other women he dated about their missing sleep turbans.

"That is fascinating and new information." I nodded. "Okay, I'll be right back."

I went to the bathroom, washed my face, brushed my teeth, and put on a tank top with sleep shorts. I hesitated before opening the door to reenter the bedroom. This had to be, without a doubt, the strangest day of my life, but also, somehow, the best. I'd met a random handsome stranger, ended up spending the day with him while going on what had to be the equivalent of five dates, and now, he was going to see me in my scarf and pajamas. This was wild.

Was I really going to do this?

I took a deep breath and pulled the bathroom door open. Mike was still in the bed and under the covers. He'd stripped down to his tank top, and I could see his jeans and t-shirt were neatly folded on the dresser.

"Oh my God," he said in an exaggerated gasp.

"What?" I bit my lip and smoothed my tank top over my waist, feeling self-conscious.

"Nothing. You look beautiful." He smiled. "Get in here." He patted the spot on the bed I'd recently vacated.

I narrowed my eyes at him and crawled into bed beside him.

"Are you sure about this?" He snaked his arm around my waist and whispered in my ear.

"Yes." I snuggled into him until my back was against his chest. My bare thighs pressed against his. "Your boxers are still damp."

"I know," he chuckled. "I'm sorry."

"You could always take them off," I suggested.

"Go to sleep, Jordyn."

"Good night, Mike."

"Good night, baby doll."

I slapped him on the thigh and felt his chest vibrate with laughter as I drifted off to sleep again.

7

WHEN I WOKE UP, it was still dark outside, and Mike, who snored, was still asleep beside me. I turned to face him and studied his chiseled features. His stubble was longer that it was when I met him less than twenty-four hours ago. I traced his thick dark eyebrows with the pad of my index finger and slid it down the bridge of his strong nose. He opened his eyes to find me tracing his bottom lip with my thumb.

"Busted," he whispered with a smile.

"Hi." I grinned at him.

"How are you feeling? Are you hungover?"

"Not at all, actually."

"See, it's the secret sauce."

"You mean the Thousand Island dressing?" I giggled.

"No, Jordyn. It's a secret." He smirked at me, and I burst out laughing.

Mike wrapped his arm around my waist, pulled me close to him, and kissed me. I draped one of my legs over his waist. He responded by sliding his thigh between my legs and rolling me onto my back while pressing himself between my open legs. He never broke the seal of our lips. The thin fabric of his boxers and my shorts did little to dampen the sensation of Mike's rolling hips pressing his erection between my sensitive folds.

He slipped a giant palm under my tank top. I felt his fingertips smooth over the delicate skin of my belly and dance across my rib cage until I felt his large hand close over one of the globes of my breasts and gently squeeze. I moaned into his mouth and writhed under him.

"Jordyn." Mike separated our lips and panted. "I have to tell you something."

"What? Now?"

"It's kind of important."

"Can it wait?" I said, and it almost sounded like a whine.

"I mean, it can, but—"

"Are you married?" I asked. He shook his head. "Do you have an STI?" Another head shake. "Are you really a serial killer?" He shook his head for a third time and tried to stifle a chuckle. "Then, I don't want to know. Not now." I grabbed his face and kissed him.

He stopped his protest and melted into our kiss. He painted my collarbone and chest with his lips and tongue as he moved down my torso. I felt him sucking on the skin of my hips. He lavished my navel with long slow licks. I froze when I felt his lips near the waistband of my shorts.

"Um, Mike?"

"Yeah, what?" He jerked his head up to face me. "Do you want me to stop?"

"No, but I should warn you—"

"Yeah, you already told me about your giant panties." He smirked.

"No, I mean I haven't been with anyone in a while and I'm way overdue for a spa appointment. It's like 1976 down there."

"Good. Was that it?" He raised his eyebrows.

"Well, I haven't showered since yesterday morning, and we did all that walking around…"

"Okay. Neither of those are deterrents." He planted a kiss on the skin above the waistband of my shorts. "Do you want this, Jordyn?"

What the hell kind of question was that?

"Yes," I answered.

"Good." He peeled my shorts down my thighs. "Whoa. These panties are huge." He grinned up at me.

"Shut up." I tapped him on the top of the head with my finger. He hooked his fingers into the elastic of my underwear and slid them down my legs until they met my shorts, which were bunched up around my ankles. He freed one foot from my panties and pajamas before spreading my thighs.

"You're beautiful everywhere," he whispered before planting a kiss on my inner thigh, eliciting a small whimper from me. He brushed a thick fingertip through my labia and parted my curls before smoothing his tongue over my crevice and the small sensitive bundle of nerves that had been craving Mike's attention. The instant his mouth touched my clit a wave of pleasure and warmth radiated through my entire body. His hands slid under my ass, lifting and holding me in position. I began to moan and roll my hips in rhythm with his gentle licks and kisses. He rolled me onto my side and lifted one of my legs in the air as he continued to explore every inch of flesh between my thighs.

"Jesus Christ, Jordyn." He rolled me onto my belly and continued to taste me as I grabbed a pillow to muffle the squeals Mike was causing. Suddenly, the pillow was pulled away. "No," he panted. "I need to hear you." He dove between my legs again. His thick stubble massaged my inner thighs and I felt Mike slide one, then two fingers inside me. The sensations were overwhelming and intense. My muscles began to tighten around his fingers and my knees started to tremble. "That's right, baby," Mike coaxed me between licks and kisses. "Come for me." As had been the custom since the moment I met him, I followed Mike's lead. Of all the wonderful places he'd taken me, this was my favorite.

"Oh my God. Oh my God." I sucked in deep breaths in an effort to tether myself to reality as I floated back down to earth.

Mike kissed his way up my belly, closed his lips over one of my nipples and bit down gently. He continued his journey across my body, planting kisses on my chest, collarbone and throat before lying on the bed next to me and turning me to face him.

"Hi," he whispered to me and smiled.

"Hi," I responded in a chuckle and smoothed my palm over his rough cheek.

"Can I kiss you?" His breath was heavy with the scent of me. His nose, lips, and cheeks were covered with a thin, glossy layer of what I knew was also me. It was the sexiest thing I'd ever seen.

"Yes." I inched forward and planted a kiss on his lips. "And you don't have to ask." Another kiss. "Or jump into fountains." Kiss. "Or complete the seven labors of Hercules." Kiss and a chuckle.

"Well, that's a relief, because there were actually twelve."

"Really?"

"Mm-hmm. I mean, I would gladly wrestle a lion for one of these." He kissed me again. "But it's a relief to know I don't have to."

"You're silly."

"I like you, Jordyn," he whispered. My heart swelled and I couldn't hold back a grin when I answered.

"I like you, too."

"I mean, I really like you. I don't want this to be a one-day thing. This has been the best not-a-date of my life, and I want more."

I smiled and I felt my eyes stinging. This felt like the perfect moment, but there was one big problem.

"But I live on the other side of the country, and I'm leaving on Tuesday."

We stared at each other in silence for a few seconds.

"But...I don't know... If things go well with my interview, I'd be moving here. You could not-date me all you want then." I expected Mike to at least smile at my joke, but instead, he wrapped a hand around my shoulder and squeezed.

"Jordyn, I really have to tell you something."

"Ugh, not this again." I rolled my eyes. "We're both alcohol-free, in this bed, and you weren't scared off by my scarf and giant underwear," I said. He grinned at me, and I traced one of his dimples with my finger. "I was kind of hoping we could…" I trailed off and waggled my eyebrows suggestively.

"I'm sorry. I would love that, but I can't."

"What do you mean, you can't?" My brain was whirring, trying to latch on to an explanation for Mike's weird behavior. "Do you have an issue with"—I pointed to his waist—"because it's fine. We can just hold each other, or I could—"

"What? No! No. I'm fine. I'm great, actually. No issue at all with that, but that's not the reason I can't be with you."

"Oh my God, you are married." I tried to sit up.

"No." Mike groaned in frustration and wiped a hand over his face. "I'm sucking at this, so I'm just gonna say it."

"Say what?" My heart was pounding.

"Mike is short for Micah."

Micah… Micah…

Why the hell did that name sound so familiar?

"Micah?" I whispered, hoping if I said it out loud, it would shake loose some memory.

"Micah…Grayson," he whispered.

Oh my God. Oh my God. Oh my fucking God.

"You flew here to interview with my company."

8

Micah fucking Grayson.

Founder and CEO of Grayson Technology.

I jumped out of bed. Mike's eyes flicked downwards, and I realized that I was still naked from the waist down. I snatched the duvet off of the bed to cover myself, revealing the giant tent Mike had pitched in his boxers. He looked down and quickly covered himself with a pillow.

"Please, tell me this is one of your jokes," I pleaded with him. "Please tell me you're lying." Deep down, I knew it was the truth. The CEO of my dream job, my escape from the well-meaning, loving, but too-watchful eyes of my parents, had his head between my legs twenty minutes ago.

"Jordyn, I'm so sorry." Mike, or Micah, or whatever the hell his name was, sat up and tried to reach for me with the hand that wasn't securing the pillow. "I tried to tell you sooner."

"You should have tried harder." I felt around the mattress for my panties and shorts. While clutching them with the hand that wasn't securing the duvet around my waist, I made a slow, silent, undignified waddle across the bedroom. After two attempts, I managed to pull the cover all the way into the bathroom and close the door with a satisfying slam.

"You better not still be here when I get out," I shouted through the door as I got dressed. I was met with silence.

I pulled on my panties and shorts before putting my palms on the bathroom counter and taking deep breaths to try and center myself. This was a nightmare. I was sure I was still sleeping. This kind of shit didn't happen in real life.

My thoughts were interrupted by a low knock.

"Jordyn." Mike's deep voice floated through the closed door. "Please. Can we talk about this?"

Micah Grayson was a liar, and also bad at following directions. I wondered if this was how he ran his company. I took a deep breath and whipped the door open.

"You wanna talk?" I asked. Mike was standing in the doorway, fully dressed.

"Yes." He nodded and took a few steps back and sat on the bed. "I don't want to leave things like this."

"Why didn't you tell me your name was Micah?"

He sighed and scratched his head. "The only people that call me Micah are my mother or business acquaintances. Everyone else calls me Mike."

"So, then I should start calling you Micah, or do you prefer Mr. Grayson?"

He gave me a wounded look that made me feel the smallest twinge of regret. He didn't answer me.

"Why isn't there a picture of you on the company's website?"

"There aren't pictures of anyone who works for the company on the website. We design video games and CGI programs for film and TV. Who gives a fuck what we look like?"

"Well, it would have been nice not to get blindsided like this." I crossed my arms, instantly aware that I'd made an incredibly flimsy argument.

"Are you serious?" He threw his hands up. "This was something I should've been prepared for? I'll bring it up at the next meeting. Everybody should have their picture on the site to prevent hooking up with gorgeous strangers in bookstores."

"No, don't do that." I wagged my finger at him. "Don't compliment me when I'm pissed at you."

"Sorry?" He shrugged and an adorable smile curled his lips, forcing me to turn away from him. I needed to hold on to my anger, but he wasn't making it easy.

"Why didn't you tell me who you were? All fucking day. I told you about my jobs and what I did."

"I did tell you who I was. I told you lots of things, Jordyn. Important things. Personal things. Things I never get to talk about with anyone else. Do you know how long it's been since I've had a conversation with someone that wasn't about work or my company? Telling the same fucking stories over and over again? I was tired of people always hitting me up for money or jobs— which I get is ironic. But, today, with you, was the first time I'd felt like myself in a long time. I didn't want to ruin it. I'm sorry."

Turning to look at Mike had been a mistake. His sad eyes pierced my heart. My anger was becoming a thin and slippery mist, sliding through my fingers as I desperately tried to hold on to it.

"You're the CEO. This is my third interview. Your company paid for me to come here. You're really gonna tell me you didn't know who I was when you met me?"

"No, of course not," he said as if I'd asked him the most absurd question. "I have an HR department. I only meet potential employees during the last phase of the interview process. Trust me, if I knew who you were, I would have stayed away...I would have tried, at least."

"So why didn't you say anything in the bar?"

"I was going to. I wanted to...but I was already..."

He trailed off and scratched his head again.

"Already what?"

"I just... I wanted more time...with you."

I sighed in frustration because Mike had made it impossible for me to stay mad at him.

"You changed the subject when I brought it up in the museum. I thought I was boring you."

"I told you, I hate talking about work." He shrugged. "And there's nothing boring about you, Jordyn."

"You went down on me. For a really long time." I'd clearly run out of arguments, but I still wanted to yell at him.

"Again…sorry?" He shrugged again. His bottom lip was tucked between his teeth and he was trying to stifle a laugh. I picked up a pillow and hit him with it. "Ow."

"I told you that I would jinx my interview if I talked about it."

"So, this is actually all *your* fault." The corners of his lips were still curled in a smirk. I hit him with the pillow again.

"What am I supposed to do now?"

"I don't know." His smile faded. "Go to the interview."

I let out a laugh.

"And do what, Mike?" I folded my arms across my chest. "Pretend I don't know what the CEO's morning breath tastes like?"

"I have morning breath?" he asked and held a palm in front of his mouth.

"Yes. And you snore," I added.

"Well, I knew that. I have a nose thing I'm supposed to wear at night but I didn't bring—"

"Excuse me," I interrupted him. "We're discussing the fact that I flew from one end of the country to the other for no damn reason!"

"Right." He nodded. "You didn't fly here for no reason. You should go to the interview."

"How?"

"Listen, I know this makes me sound like a giant asshole, but I really hope you don't get the job," he continued after catching my glare, "but I won't stand in your way."

"What do you mean?"

"I mean, I'm not gonna say anything to anyone about this—us, and we'll see what happens."

"And what happens if I get the job?"

"We sign a disclosure form and avoid each other like the plague."

"And if I don't?"

"Then I spend a lot of time and money flying back and forth to New York to try to convince you to forgive me and give me a second chance."

The last bit of my anger with him melted away at his words, but I still felt hollow inside.

"This is so fucked up." I collapsed on the bed next to him and put my head on his shoulder.

"Yeah," he agreed and dropped a kiss on my head, making me sigh.

"Why didn't you tell me you were a tech prodigy genius?"

Mike let out a low chuckle. "Because I'm not a tech prodigy genius. I'm a guy with a knack for computers and an expensive education, who had a good idea and parents that could give him two hundred and fifty grand to start a company."

"That wasn't an Uber driver that picked us up, was it?"

"No." He put his arm around my waist. "That was my driver, Steve. You think I would leave you asleep in the back seat of a car with a stranger?"

"I guess not." I heaved a deep sigh. "Well, for what it's worth, and whatever happens tomorrow, I had a really great time yesterday."

"Just yesterday?" he asked with a raised eyebrow that made my belly flutter.

"And this morning." I smiled at him.

"Me, too," he whispered. "You're incredible, Jordyn."

His palm slid across my cheek and he tilted my head up to meet his lips. I closed my eyes.

"Mike," I whispered.

"Yeah?" His warm breath caressed my cheek.

"I think I should revoke the blanket consent for kisses." I opened my eyes to find his brown ones gazing at me, filled with disappointment.

"Yeah." He sighed. "You're probably right. I should go."

I wanted to tell him to stay, but I bit my lip instead and watched him get to his feet and walk towards the bedroom door. He wrapped his hand around the knob before turning to face me.

"Please promise me you'll go to the interview."

"Can I promise you that I'll think about it?"

"Jordyn, I could figure out a way to get over you, but I could never forgive myself if I fucked this up for you. Please, go."

I forced myself to look at him, and his sad expression made my eyes sting with tears. I closed my eyes and nodded.

"Thank you." He left the bedroom and closed the door behind him. A few seconds later, I heard him leave the apartment. I flopped onto the bed and let myself cry.

9

I WAS LYING in the same spot on the bed with my feet dangling off the mattress hours later when I heard my phone ring. I instantly knew it was my mother, but a small part of me hoped it was Mike calling before I remembered that I'd never given him my number.

"Hey, Mom."

"Hey, California girl! Are you having fun? I thought you'd be out sightseeing, but I haven't seen any new posts on your Instagram. I hope you're not sitting in your hotel room reading books and ordering pizza."

I took a deep breath and let it out slowly. I tried to remember how much my parents loved me and that my mom had no idea that I'd spent the morning crying in a heap in my pajamas over a relationship that lasted one day and possibly jeopardized my entire reason for coming here in the first place.

"No, I saw some cool stuff yesterday."

"And you didn't take any pictures? That's not like you. Are you wearing sunscreen?"

"Yes."

"Well, don't get friendly with any strangers or tell anyone you're traveling by yourself."

Too late.

"I won't."

"Good. Are you ready for your interview?"

No.

"Yes."

"That's my girl. You have copies of your CV printed out? I know you kids do digital everything but it never hurts to have hard copy backups…in case of a blackout or something—"

Jesus Christ. A blackout, Mom? Really?

"And you did thorough research on the company? Of course, you did, but I read that the CEO started the company when he was only twenty-three. If your interview goes well—and it will, because you're my daughter—and you get to meet him, you should definitely bring that up. These young tech CEO types love to talk about how smart they are—"

Not this young tech CEO.

"And make sure you ask your interviewer questions about the company. Make it clear that they need you, not the other way around. I hope you took my advice and decided to wear a suit to the interview. I know it's fashionable these days to go to work in your pajamas, but it is always a good idea to make a good first impression. Jordyn?"

My parents were in their mid-sixties, and despite knowing all the latest advancements in medical technology were woefully ignorant of how the world works for people in their twenties. My mother stopped speaking to me for a week after I deleted my Facebook account and only got an Instagram account to keep track of me.

"Jordyn?" she repeated. "Are you still there? These damn phones… Derrick!"

"Mom."

"Derrick," she yelled for my dad again, "try calling Jordyn on your phone!"

"Mom! I'm still here."

"Oh, there you are... Never mind!" she screamed, and I had to hold my phone away from my ear.

"Are you okay, pumpkin?" she asked. "You sound a little sad."

"I'm fine," I lied. "I guess I'm just a little nervous about the interview." I sighed. "And a little bit nervous about what would happen after the interview."

"What do you mean?"

"What if I don't get it?"

"Then you don't get it. You apply for something else and keep going until you do get something."

"And what if I get it and I hate it?"

"Then you apply for something else and keep going until you get something you don't hate. This doesn't sound like you. Is there something else you're not telling me?"

Yes.

"No. I'm also suffering from jet lag. I'm gonna use today to relax, let my body adjust and prep for the interview."

"Good girl. Your dad and I love you so much, and we're so proud of you."

"Thanks, Mom. I love you too."

"Do you have enough money?"

"Yes, Mom. I'm hanging up."

I heard my dad's voice in the background. "What happened? Why does she need money?"

"Bye, Mom. Give Daddy a kiss for me!"

"Bye, pumpkin."

I peeled myself out of bed and went to the bedroom window. I snapped a photo of the sky and posted it to my Instagram feed with the caption:

A ROOM WITH A VIEW.

I tried explaining to my parents the concept of an Airbnb, but they kept getting stuck on the idea of my staying in a stranger's apartment, so I told them I was staying in a hotel.

A couple seconds after I posted the picture, I got two notifications.

JordynsDrMomma liked your photo.

JordynsDrMomma commented: So beautiful!!! It looks like a postcard!!! Love you!!!

I smiled and shook my head before tapping the magnifying glass icon. I took a deep breath and typed in Mike's name, his real name.

———

Micah Grayson

Entrepreneur

Founder and CEO of Grayson Technology

It's all fun and games

Grayson.Technology

———

He had over fifty-thousand followers, and there were no pictures of his face, or any people, for that matter. It was mostly videos, product launches, and abstract photos. It didn't feel like the person I had spent the last day with.

I typed "Mike Grayson" in the search bar and a bunch of results came up. I scrolled for a while, and almost gave up hope until I saw a profile photo of a close-up of a smile with an incredibly familiar dimple. I'd been memorizing that smile for the past twenty-four hours. I clicked on the profile.

MIKE (HE/HIM/HIS)

BROTHER. SON. FRIEND. LARGE CHILD. MASTER OF DISGUISE. I STOLE YOUR SANDWICH FROM THE BREAK ROOM FRIDGE.

IT WAS DEFINITELY HIM. He had eighty-seven followers and the account was set to private. I almost sent a follow request but thought better of it.

I closed the app, tossed my phone on the bed, and decided to start my day.

———

MY DAY CONSISTED OF A SHOWER, ordering Door-Dash for breakfast, lunch, and dinner, reading *White Whiskey Bargain, Pink Slip, Everything She Never Wanted* and starting to re-read *Indigo* before I had to stop because it made me miss Mike too much. I thought about taking a walk around the neighborhood but decided it would be too depressing, and I didn't want to risk running into the mayor of Culver City.

I climbed into bed and hugged the pillow that smelled like a sweaty, snoring goofball and wondered if Mike was thinking about me, wherever he was tonight. I wondered if he was dancing in the fountain for someone else.

————

GRAYSON TECHNOLOGY WAS AS LAID-BACK as I suspected. I could feel Mike's personality everywhere in the space. My heart was pounding out of my chest because I kept expecting him to appear around every corner.

I had dressed in a white button-up blouse with a dark navy blue blazer over a pair of skinny jeans and black-and-white Adidas. I sent my mom a selfie from the waist up and was almost tempted to send her a photo of one of the guys I passed, sitting in a beanbag chair, typing on a laptop wearing a giant pair of headphones and pajama pants.

The interview started with a standard programming test. It was easier than I expected it to be, and it felt good to immerse myself in something that made sense after my very confusing weekend.

"So, what do you think of the offices, Jordyn?" Chris, my interviewer, asked once we were seated in their office.

"They're great. I love the diversity of workspaces and the idea of being able to sit at a desk when I want to and no one's gonna look at me sideways if I need to sit on the floor."

"That is our CEO. He's all about making everyone who works for him feel comfortable and valued. He says it fuels creativity and productivity." They smiled.

I felt my stomach lurch. This morning, I somehow tricked myself into believing that there was the tiniest possibility that this was all a big misunderstanding, and I was interviewing at a different Grayson Technology run by a different Micah

Grayson, but walking around his offices and hearing Chris talk about him made it real. They were describing the man that I'd spent the weekend falling for, and this was his company.

Chris' computer pinged with an alert.

"Wow! I got the results from your programming test and—don't quote me—but this might be one of the highest scores I've ever seen. Speed, accuracy. Nicely done."

"Thanks. Ruby and Python are my love languages." I shrugged and smiled at them.

"Love languages! I like that. You're funny." Chris smiled before tapping on their keyboard.

"So, you did a video conference with Regina last month, and she had nothing but great things to say about you. I've met you, and I think you'll do nicely here. You'll be relocating from New York?"

"Yes."

"Okay. We can definitely help with that. And let's discuss salary. I think you'll be a great addition to the team and we try to be competitive here, so we are prepared to offer you"—they scribbled on a Post-it and handed it to me—"this."

I took a deep breath and unfolded the note. They'd written a figure that was more than what I'd made at my last job, and while it wasn't as much as I was hoping for, I'd be able to easily afford to live on my own in Culver City.

"Is everything okay?"

"Yes," I stammered, but I couldn't stop staring at the paper. I was hoping for some reason or excuse to not take the job, but I didn't have one, not a logical one, anyway.

"Look." Chris sighed, sensing my disappointment, but not knowing the reason. "I know it may not be what you were expecting, and Culver City is a wildly expensive place to live, but, Jordyn, you're really talented. This is the best we can offer right now, but this is a really welcoming bunch of people and I'm sure we can help you figure out a way to make it work."

"Thank you." I smiled and nodded.

"Well, usually this is the part where I introduce you to our CEO—"

My heart sped up and I began taking slow calming breaths. I looked to the door of Chris' office, expecting Mike to walk through it.

"—but he took a rare personal day today, so I will have to catch him up on everything tomorrow. But we'll need a decision from you in a week, sooner if you can swing it."

"Thank you."

10

My Uber, which was actually an Uber, passed the bookstore on the way back to the apartment. I was hit by a sudden urge to go inside, but I restrained myself.

The interview had gone better than expected, but I knew in my gut that I wouldn't be able to work so close to Mike.

Grayson Technology paid for three food trucks to park outside the offices and provide free lunches for its employees. Chris encouraged me to take something to go after my interview. So, I ordered something from each truck.

Back at the apartment, I decided to skip the grilled cheese and bacon sandwich and the fish tacos and go straight for the bag of beignets. After artfully arranging them on a plate, I snapped a photo, adjusted the settings, and posted it to my feed with the caption:

LA Beignet. #TheBeignetTruck

After taking the first bite, I closed my eyes and moaned, it was so good. My fingers were already greasy and my blazer was covered in powdered sugar, but I didn't care. Right on schedule, there were two alerts:

JordynsDrMomma liked your photo.

JordynsDrMomma commented: Ooooo, those look so good! I haven't had a good beignet since Essencefest in 2009. @CookieTurner193 Remember those beignets we had at that place in New Orleans.

A few seconds later:

CookieTurner193 commented: @JordynsDrMomma Yes, girl. I still think about those beignets. We have to go back. Hey, Jordyn! Good luck on your interview!

I shook my head and snorted a laugh. My mom had tagged my aunt Cookie, whose name was actually

Sandra, in the comments, and those two would probably chat back and forth in my mentions before calling each other on the phone and talking for three hours.

My thoughts drifted to Mike, and I wondered why he hadn't come to work. If this was his plan to avoid me, what would he do if I accepted the position?

"We sign a disclosure form and avoid each other like the plague."

I typed his Instagram handle into the search bar and almost dropped my phone when I saw that his profile was no longer set to private. He'd also changed his bio:

MIKE (HE/HIM/HIS)

BROTHER. SON. FRIEND. LARGE CHILD. MASTER OF DISGUISE. KISS THIEF. HOPEFUL ROMANTIC.

The latest post in the top left corner of the grid was the video I recorded of him dancing in the fountain. I'd already seen that live and was way too curious about what other things Mike would post on his feed. I scrolled through pictures of him with his friends, gorgeous pictures of LA, and vacation photos from all around the world. There were pictures of his family. The Graysons took glamorous, Kardashian-style holiday photos every year and Mike looked almost exactly like his father, but he had his mother's dark hair and eyes. Laura, while gorgeous, more closely resembled Mike and their dad. Erica looked like a carbon copy of their mom, who didn't look like she'd aged much since her pageant days. There were throwback pictures of Mike's grandmother, and an adorable photo of Mike when he was about five or six in full makeup, wearing a pageant crown and a sash.

As I scrolled through the entire feed—yes, the entire feed—I hardly saw any mention of Mike's company, or the fact that Mike's family was really rich. When I reached the bottom, I saw that most of the first twenty or so pictures were of pairs of expensive sneakers. I smiled to myself. Mike was a reformed sneakerhead. I tapped to expand the photo and was attempting to scroll down to see the date when a giant white heart quickly flashed on my phone screen.

Shit. Shit. Shit.

Did I like that picture?

I did.

I just liked a six-year-old Instagram photo.

I couldn't unlike it because he would still get a notification. I picked up a second beignet and shoved it in my mouth, hoping to quell the embarrassment of getting caught cyberstalking my potential new boss. It was starting to work when I saw I had another notification.

MIKEGRAYSON4 STARTED FOLLOWING YOU.

MIKEGRAYSON4 WANTS TO SEND YOU A MESSAGE.

I opened the message from Mike. It was one word:

BUSTED.

I rolled my eyes and laughed.

I responded with a gif of Dave Chapelle knocking over a pitcher of water as a distraction and running away.

Mike responded almost immediately.

COME TO THE BOOKSTORE.

I sighed and stared at my phone's screen before typing:

I DON'T THINK THAT'S A GOOD IDEA.

Another immediate response came.

It's a very bad idea, but I'm gonna wait there all day until you show up.

––––––

I took another bite of my beignet while I thought about what I was going to do. I went back to Mike's feed and clicked on the video. He was dancing half-naked in the fountain to cheers and applause. The phone was shaking so badly, and I could hear myself screeching with laughter.

Ugh, is that really what my laugh sounds like?

The video ended with Mike walking out of the fountain towards the camera, shaking himself dry like a dog. I read the video's caption:

Best Three Years of My Life

Saturday was the best three years of my life too.

Dammit, Mike. Of course, I'm gonna go to the bookstore.

I finished my beignet, liked the post, and left a comment.

See you soon.

————

I RAN to the bookstore and threw the door open, panting and out of breath. Mike had his back turned when I walked in, and he was talking to a woman. My heart thudded and stopped. I was contemplating backing out of the store when I recognized her as the woman who was working at the store the day we met. She pointed at me and Mike turned to look.

His face lit up and he took long strides to close the distance between us.

"Hi," he said and grinned.

"Hi," I replied, before I saw his smile falter.

"Aw, man. I missed beignet day?"

"What? How did you—"

His eyes flicked to my blazer that was lightly dusted with powdered sugar. I looked down and smiled, noticing that I hadn't done the best job dusting myself off before I ran out of the apartment.

"They're pretty good." I shrugged.

"I can tell." He smiled and reached to wipe my face before pausing. "May I?"

I nodded, and Mike brushed his thumb across my cheek. His touch radiated warmth to every part of my body.

"Thank you," I whispered.

"Thank you for coming."

"So...why did you want me to meet you here?"

"Well, I missed you."

I was dying to tell him that I missed him, too, but instead, I said, "Is that why you didn't come to the office?"

He nodded. "I was also working on an important project, which is the other reason I wanted you to meet me."

"Okay?"

Mike took a deep breath and wiped a hand over his face. "I wanna fight for you, Jordyn."

"What?" I spluttered. "Fight for me?"

"Yeah. I heard about your interview. Chris has called me three times. They sent me your programming test scores and want me to sign off on a higher salary offer in case you try to turn down the job."

Whoa. I hadn't realized the interview went that well.

"So, why are you telling me this? This is good, right?"

"Not for me." He reached up and scratched the back of his head. "I'm really trying to be a good guy here but I know I couldn't handle seeing you in the office and not being with you. I even asked my lawyer about the legal ramifications of dating an employee."

"And?"

"She said that it technically wasn't illegal, but was incredibly ill-advised."

"So, my options are one, accept my dream job at GrayTech—which I now know I can negotiate a higher salary for—while making both of us miserable or risking an HR nightmare, and two, go home to New York without a job and put thousands of miles between us."

"What if there was a third option?"

"I'm listening."

"Chris gave you a week to accept the position?"

I nodded.

"Why don't you stay in Culver City and keep looking for a different job? If you find something better, awesome. If you don't, take the job at GrayTech."

A hysterical chuckle bubbled out of my chest at Mike's suggestion.

"A week? Seriously. Do you know how long it took me to get *this* interview? And you expect me to find something else—something better—in a week."

Mike had gone oddly quiet and was wearing a guilty expression.

"What?" I asked and narrowed my eyes.

"I might have emailed a couple of my friends and sent them your CV."

"Might have?"

"You have two interviews next week," he said in a sigh. His phone pinged in his pocket. He pulled it out and checked the screen. "Three."

"Mike, seriously." I crossed my arms over my chest and glared at him. "That is some serious alphahole bullshit."

"I know, but I had to do something. I've never felt this way about anyone before. I can't let you go without knowing that I tried everything."

"You should have asked me first."

"I know." He bit his bottom lip, and his eyes seemed to be searching my face for a reaction. I know I should have been more upset at him, but I wasn't. I wanted the job at GrayTech, but I wanted Mike more, which didn't make sense. No amount of logical reasoning would justify giving up the opportunity of a lifetime for a man who'd spent a day sweeping me off my feet.

I uncrossed my arms and walked to a couch that was sitting in the middle of the store and sank into it. I stared at a colorful display of floating books, suspended from the ceiling and tried to make sense of the last three days. This wasn't an algorithm I could search for errors. This was real and messy and confusing. Mike followed me and lowered himself onto the cushion next to me. We sat in silence for a few moments before he moved closer to me.

"Hey, talk to me. Tell me what you're thinking." He smoothed his palm over my back and flooded my chest with warmth.

"I've probably read a hundred books where this exact thing happens and now it's happening to me and I don't know how to feel."

"Same. I was raised by people this exact thing happened to and I'm just as confused."

"We're not in love, right?" I wasn't sure if I was talking to Mike or myself.

"I don't know if we're in love, but I know whenever I'm with you, I'm really happy, and when I'm not with you, I'm really sad." He tapped me on the shoulder and I turned to look at him. "Jordyn, I don't like being sad."

I snorted a laugh and shook my head.

"We barely know each other."

"I don't know if I agree with that, but you could spend a week getting to know me while you go to interviews." He raised a hopeful eyebrow.

"If I went on those interviews, I'd be condoning your terrible behavior."

"I would do a million terrible things for you, baby doll."

I smiled at him.

"Well, my flight leaves tomorrow, and I'd have to find another place to stay."

"Reschedule your flight and stay with me."

"I'm not moving in with you."

"Whoa, calm down. We've only known each other for three days. My parents were dating for five days before they moved in together. Let's not jump the gun."

"You are such a goofball." I placed my hand on his cheek, which was now covered in the beginnings of a beard, threatening to bury my dimples. Mike leaned closer.

"Is that a good thing?" He pressed our foreheads together.

Mike's proposition offered the perfect solution. I flew to California hoping to start over in a new city. That didn't hinge on my working for one particular company. If life is an unpredictable leap of faith, then new Jordyn was ready to jump.

"I don't know. Let's see how this week goes."

His face spread into a wide grin. "Really?"

I nodded and rubbed our noses together.

"Mike?"

"Yes, Jordyn?"

"I'm reinstating my blanket consent for kisses."

My real life book boyfriend huffed out a chuckle and pressed our lips together. He pulled away after a few moments and licked his lips.

"I love beignet day."

THE END

EPILOGUE

JORDYN WAS STILL ASLEEP when I woke up. I watched her for a few minutes, like I did almost every morning, before I pulled out my nose clip and went to the kitchen to attempt to make breakfast.

Within twenty minutes, I managed to burn everything and set off the smoke alarm, which caused her to run into the kitchen still wearing her silk turban—a gift from my mom—and one of my t-shirts.

"Baby." She coughed. "What in the hell…" She waved the smoke away from her face before grabbing the broom from the closet and fanning the smoke alarm until the beeping stopped.

She was trying to stifle a laugh when I walked up to her, lifted her onto the kitchen counter and kissed her.

"Happy one-year anniversary." I shrugged, making her snort laugh and kiss me again.

"How did you grow up in a house with four women and never learn to cook?"

"That's sexist." I nuzzled her neck with my nose, inhaling the scent of the remnants of her face cream. "And we had a chef."

"I'm gonna order waffles." She scooted off the counter with a faint squeaking sound and ran into our bedroom to grab her phone.

I quickly scraped the burnt eggs and bacon into the trash and walked into our bathroom to find her brushing her teeth. I grabbed my toothbrush.

"Hey, do you have to work today?" I said as I was squeezing toothpaste onto my brush.

"No, you asked me to take today off." She leaned over and spit into the sink and turned on the faucet.

After getting two competitive job offers, Jordyn ended up at Logiq, a company that designs music software, run by one of my old CalTech classmates, a ballbuster who never misses an opportunity to thank me for not hiring Jordyn myself.

We'd been living together ever since.

"Did you order waffles yet?" I asked after I spit my mouthwash into the sink.

"No, I was waiting for you." She smiled as she walked past me.

I grabbed a handful of her ass and followed her out of the bathroom. She spun to face me, grabbed my collar, pulled me down for a kiss, and walked me towards the bed.

"I love you." She looked up at me as she inched backwards onto the bed.

"I love you, too." I pulled her t-shirt off and crawled on top of her. She pulled her silk cap off to reveal a cascade of shiny dark brown curls.

"Come here." She crooked a finger at me and I moved over her, planting a kiss on every square inch of her perfect body until our lips met.

"Hey, I've been thinking…"

"I thought I smelled something burning." She narrowed her eyes and grinned at me.

"That was breakfast." I tickled her. "Listen, what if… we didn't use a condom today?"

She raised an eyebrow, but she didn't look upset.

"Or tonight, or tomorrow…" I continued.

"Mike, do you wanna try for a baby?"

"Yes. Do you want to try for a baby?" I searched her face for a reaction. She was gazing up at me, wearing one of her mischievous smiles, but she still hadn't answered me.

"Jordyn?"

"Do you think we're ready for a baby?"

I nodded and kissed her.

"Okay." She reached up and traced one of my dimples with her finger.

"Really?"

"Really."

I lowered myself onto her and covered her neck and collarbone with kisses. Jordyn tangled her fingers in my hair as I moved down her body. I sucked one of her dark brown nipples into my mouth and pressed my teeth into the pebbled bud, making her moan. I loved moving over her, teasing, tantalizing, and exploring; playing her body like an instrument of pleasure.

After I'd made her come with my mouth and fingers, I freed myself from my boxers and slid into her slowly, the way I knew she wanted. Jordyn coiled herself around my body and rocked her hips in synergy with my thrusts. She felt so good, and I couldn't believe she was mine. The instant I saw her in that bookstore, I knew she was special, and the more time I spent with her, the more I knew I couldn't let her go.

"Fuck, Jordyn. I fucking love you so much." I clutched fistfuls of our sheets, trying to hold on for a little bit longer and delay the inevitable. She arched her back and moaned in response. She began spasming, and I couldn't hold on. I exploded into her, rode the waves of her orgasm and collapsed on top of her, sweaty and exhausted. She wrapped her arms around my back and placed a delicate kiss on my nose.

"Hey, babe."

"Yes, gorgeous?"

"I think I'm pregnant."

"I don't think it works that fast," I mumbled into her chest.

She giggled. "No, I think it worked in the coat closet at your parents' anniversary party."

I picked my head up and looked at her.

"Are you serious?"

"Yeah. We didn't use a condom that night, and this month, my period was late, so I took about four tests, and they were all positive."

I sat up and placed a trembling hand over her belly as if I'd be able to feel something moving inside.

"When was this?" I asked.

"Last week."

"When were you gonna tell me?"

"I was saving it for an anniversary surprise, but then you said you wanted to try for a baby..." She shrugged.

"Why didn't you tell me when I just asked you if you wanted to try for a baby?"

"I wanted to have sex first." She shrugged again.

"I remember doing something similar and getting my kissing privileges revoked." I rolled onto my back and slid her onto my chest.

"I don't make the rules." She grabbed my face and kissed me. "But I still have to go to the doctor, confirm the results, and wait to hear a heartbeat."

My heart was pounding in my chest. Jordyn was pregnant, and I was the father. I was going to be a father. I wanted to scream from excitement. I wanted to cry because I was gonna have a kid that Lola and Abuela would never meet. I wanted to call my parents and Erica. I wanted to hire an architect to start designing a nursery for the office. I wanted to wrap Jordyn in bubble wrap and hire a security detail and a doctor to follow her around twenty-four seven. Mostly, I wanted to hold the mother of our child in my arms and kiss her. So that's how we spent the rest of the morning.

———

"So, what's your plan for today?" she asked as she dug through her drawer for a t-shirt.

I watched Jordyn dress and stared at her flat belly, imagining how beautiful she would look swollen and pregnant.

"It's been exactly one year since we met, so I figured we'd recreate our first date."

"Does that include getting felt up in a movie theater?"

"Whatever the lady wants."

"Will you run around Monty in your underwear again?"

"I was hoping we could skip that part." I grinned at her.

"Boo." She wrapped her arms around my neck and stood on her tiptoes to kiss me. "That was my second favorite part."

"Second?" I asked when our lips parted. "What was the first?"

She raised a suggestive eyebrow at me and smiled.

"Well," I bent down, slid my palms under her thighs and hoisted her onto my waist before walking towards our bed. "We don't have to wait for the end of the night for that."

———

MY HEART WAS STILL POUNDING when I opened the door to the bookstore and led Jordyn inside.

"It's empty today." She looked around. "But I see the manager's here." Jordyn smiled and pointed to the two owners, one of whom was holding a small brown and white fluffy dog: the manager.

"I guess it's a slow day." I smiled as we passed the counter where they were standing. One of them gave me a quick nod and my pulse quickened.

Jordyn was picking up books, examining the covers and replacing them on the shelf.

"What are you thinking?"

"I don't know. It's like being hungry and then not knowing what to order when you get to the restaurant because everything on the menu looks so good." She turned to me and grinned. "Maybe I'm hungry. Can we go to Public School and come back?"

"I have a full day of stuff planned, so why don't we find a couple of books now?"

"Okay." She shot me a suspicious look. "Well, help me decide."

"*A Duke by Default?*" I suggested.

"Already read it... Wait, you haven't read that one?"

I shook my head. "Nope."

"It's over. I'm moving out." She giggled and kissed me. I started our pile of books.

"*Rafe: A Buff Male Nanny?*" I held up another book.

"Yes! But strictly for research purposes." She grinned at me.

"Don't you want to read the blurb first?"

She looked at the cover again. "Nope. Put it in the pile." She smiled, and I narrowed my eyes at her.

"Here's one called *Daddy.*" I grinned at her. She took the book from me and read the blurb.

"I don't think you're gonna find much parenting advice in this one, but we're taking it."

"*Cherishing the Goddess?*" I held up another book.

"I love the cover. That title is ridiculous. Read the blurb."

"Billionaire Alexander Wolfe—" I began.

"Ugh, billionaires. Gross." She smirked at me.

"Hey!" I frowned at her. "You're about to have a billionaire's baby."

"About to have a billionaire's baby? That's a great title. We should write that down and send it to Harlequin." She laughed. When she saw I was narrowing my eyes at her earlier comment, she laughed even harder.

She stood on her tiptoes to give me a *sorry not sorry* kiss, and I knocked over our small pile of books while she was distracted.

"Shit. Let me get that." I took a deep breath and lowered myself to one knee before looking up at her.

"Mike?"

I sucked in another deep breath and blew it out slowly, trying to focus and remember the speech I'd planned. I'd dreamed of this moment practically since the day I met her, and now that it was here, I wanted it to be perfect. I was going to tell this kind, sexy, and funny genius how much every day of the last year meant to me and how lucky I was to have her in my life.

"Jordyn, I didn't believe in love at first sight until—"

"Yes!" she screamed.

"What?"

"Yes. You're asking me to marry you, right? Or did you really bend down to pick up the books?"

"Well, no. I mean, yes," I stammered, "I am asking you… I was going to ask—"

"Yes, I'll marry you."

"Yes?" I asked. That was a lot easier than I thought it would be. A small part of me was actually worried she might say no, but the look on her face melted all doubts.

"Yes!" she repeated.

I screamed, jumped to my feet, grabbed her around the waist, and spun her around before remembering she was probably carrying our baby, set her down, and gently patted her belly. "Shit. Sorry, babe."

"Shut up, I'm fine. I'm engaged. I'm engaged!"

"She said yes!" I screamed to the empty store.

"Baby, who are you— Mom?"

Jordyn's parents, my parents, and my sister emerged from wherever they were hiding in the store and surrounded us. My mother rushed towards us, grabbed my fiancée's bare left hand and shook it at me.

"Micah, where's the ring?" she demanded.

Shit. I was so excited I forgot I had it. I dug around in my pocket for the ring my mother spent three months helping me design and presented it to Jordyn.

"That is a huge diamond. Is that real?" she gasped.

"Of course, it's real, sweetheart," Mom said. "Only the best for my daughter-in-law." She grinned at us, and I saw she had tears in her eyes.

Dad gently pulled her away from us, wrapped her in his arms and kissed her.

"If it's too big, we can trade it in for a smaller one," I whispered, and kissed Jordyn's temple when we were out of Mom's earshot. It was a four-carat cushion-cut diamond. The ring was ridiculously expensive and completely impractical for a programmer, but it was worth every penny to see the look on Jordyn's face as she gazed at it.

"Well, you already got this one." She shrugged, still not taking her eyes off the ring. "So, we might as well keep it." She shot me a giant grin and kissed me, before running into her parents' arms.

"I have no idea what that woman sees in you, but if you ever get divorced, I'm on Team Jordyn."

"Good to know." I put my arm around Erica's shoulder and gave her a kiss on the cheek.

"Congratulations, Mike. You deserve this."

"Thanks. I wish Lola was here to see it."

"What makes you think she isn't?"

This was usually the point where I teased her about the new age-y, spiritual hippie phase she was in, but this time, I was curious.

"What do you mean?"

"Do you think it's a coincidence you met the love of your life while hanging out in a romance bookstore when you and Laura were so obsessed with sappy love stories?" She raised her eyebrow in question before turning in Jordyn's direction. "I hope I'm next," she called over her shoulder.

———

AFTER A BIG LUNCH at Public School 310, we spent the rest of the day reenacting the more PG aspects of our first date with our families before dropping Jordyn's parents off at the Culver.

My hopefully pregnant fiancée and I spent the rest of the night making love. Afterwards, I stared at the ceiling, thinking about what Erica had said to me in the bookstore while Jordyn drifted off in my arms.

"Mike," she said in a sleepy mumble, "if this baby is a girl, we should definitely name her Laura."

"I think that's a great idea." I dropped a kiss on her head.

"Good night, goofball."

"Good night, baby doll."

BONUS EPILOGUE: VEGAS, BABY!
PART I: MIKE

I'D BEEN SITTING in my office for fifteen minutes, reliving my goodbye kiss with my very pregnant bride-to-be before our driver, Steve, took her to my mother's house for her latest dress fitting. The wedding was in less than two weeks, but it wasn't coming fast enough for me. Plus, I worried about Jordyn's stress levels. She's gone down to part-time at Logiq, but she takes a lot of work home.

A ping from my phone pulled me out of thoughts. It was a text message from my sister, Erica.

RIC: HEY! HAVE YOU HEARD FROM JORDYN?

ME: NO. I'M AT THE OFFICE. SHE'S SUPPOSED TO BE WITH YOU.

Ric: Well, obviously she isn't, dipshit. She said she had to go to the bathroom, then she disappeared.

What the fuck?

This was what kept me up at night. Jordyn was one of the strongest, smartest, and most capable people I knew. It was one of the millions of reasons why I loved her so much. She was also stubborn and hated to ask for help, something that drove me up the wall.

I tapped the icon with my sister's picture and put my cell to my ear.

"How exactly did you lose my fiancée?" I was simultaneously typing a message to Minerva, one of my assistants, asking her to cancel my day.

"I didn't lose her. She had the dress on, she said she had to pee. She's extremely pregnant, so it made sense. She said she didn't need any help but, after fifteen minutes, I went to check on her and she was gone."

"Is the car still there?" I grabbed my keys off my desk and walked past Minerva, who looked confused because I'd just arrived at work.

"Yup. I looked in all the obvious places, but this house is too fucking big."

"I know where she is. Don't sweat it. I'm on my way." I ended the call and stopped by one of the food trucks outside for reinforcements.

———

ABOUT A HALF-HOUR LATER, my mother, my sister, and a very perplexed wedding gown designer greeted me at the door of my childhood home in Calabasas.

"She's fine." I kissed Mom on the cheek.

"If she doesn't like the dress, we can change it." My mother sighed and tapped on her chin with one of her long manicured fingernails. It was something she did when she was nervous.

"I'm sure the dress is fine, Ma. Let me talk to her."

———

I WALKED down a deserted corridor in the South wing of the house and knocked on a closet door. I tried the handle and found that it was locked.

Jackpot.

"*Jordyn?*" I said in a sing-song voice.

"Go away. You're not supposed to see me. It's bad luck."

"*It's beignet day.*" I shook the bag. A minute later, I heard the lock click.

I slid into the coat closet before closing and locking the door behind me. The love of my life sat on the floor in the corner in a giant pile of white tulle and lace. She looked like an angel floating on a cloud.

"Hey, gorgeous." I smiled down at her.

"I feel like Jabba the Hutt in a first communion dress." She pouted, and I stifled a laugh. I sat down next to her and handed her the greasy paper bag. Our fingertips brushed when she accepted the bag, making me realize how much I'd missed her since this morning.

"Thank you," she said with a mouth full of beignet.

"You're welcome, and if Jabba the Hutt looked like this, that movie would've ended a lot differently." I leaned over and planted a kiss on the side of her head. We sat in silence for a few minutes. The mountain of white fabric she wore spilled into my lap. "This is a lot of dress, though."

"It's too small." She sniffled, fished another beignet out of the bag, and fed me a bite before eating the rest.

"Well, isn't that the point of a dress fitting?" I sucked the powdered sugar off one of her fingers.

"It fit last week. What if the designer fixes it this week and then on the morning of the wedding it's too small?"

"Then you'll have to marry me naked. You won't get any complaints from me." I grinned at her.

She snorted a chuckle and elbowed me in the ribs.

"Seriously."

"I'm serious. Dress or no dress, Jordyn Robbins. You are becoming my wife." I wrapped my hand around her neck and pulled her in for a kiss. She tasted like heaven dipped in powdered sugar. A few blissful moments of making out with Jordyn, I separated our lips with a soft pop. I almost forgot that I had to leave work before the day started, and use beignets to bribe my way into a closet she'd locked herself in.

"Talk to me, gorgeous. What's going on?"

"This wedding is huge." She did a perfect impression of the yikes emoji.

"I thought you wanted a huge wedding."

"I thought I did too. I mean, I still do… I think? I don't know. I guess I'm a little overwhelmed." Her helpless smile made my heart crack a little.

"Well," I shifted her to face me. "You're planning this *huge* wedding, you're killing it at Logiq, and every second of the day, you are growing a tiny little human in your body."

"I'm not so sure about the tiny part." She smoothed a palm over her belly under the layers of fabric.

"Yeah, that is a Grayson in there. We make gigantic babies."

She gave me a smile that lit up her entire face before she leaned forward and kissed me again.

"I love you," she whispered.

"I love you too," I replied. Jordyn's gaze dropped to my mouth and I kissed her again.

"Thank you for coming. I feel kind of silly for running off in the middle of the fitting. It just got to be too much...I'm so sorry. Was Maria upset?"

"Baby, it's okay. Mom is fine. She and Erica were a little worried about you, but no one's upset."

She let out a sigh of relief and snuggled into my chest. I smoothed my fingertips over her back, exposed by the open zipper of the dress. She moaned contentedly, making my chest vibrate.

"Hey, do you remember what happened the last time we were in this closet?" she purred.

"Yes," I planted a kiss on her head, "if I remember correctly, two of us walked in here, and when we walked out, there were three of us."

"Mmm-hmm," she said in a low hum of agreement that sent blood rushing to my dick. That's how little it took to get me turned on by my pregnant fiancée these days.

"Babe, do you have a closet fetish?" I turned my body to face her and smoothed my palm over her breasts over the dress's bodice.

"No," she laughed. "I'm overrun with pregnancy hormones, and every time I'm near my *sexy as fuck* fiancé, I want to have sex with him."

"Either one works for me." I kissed her and pulled out my phone.

"What are you doing?" she asked in between kisses.

"I'm texting Erica to tell her that you're okay and to reschedule the fitting." I didn't wait for my sister's response before I laid Jordyn on her back and started the laborious task of finding her under all the fabric. "I know I don't have a say in this, but I'm not a fan of this dress."

"Me neither." She laughed and pawed at the layers of the skirt to help me. "Don't tell your mom."

"Gorgeous, I'm not thinking about my mom right now." I slid my palms over her thighs as my head disappeared under the lace. "Whoa, these panties are huge."

"Mike, I swear, I will suffocate you with this dress," she said in a half-laugh, half moan.

"I would die a very happy man." I tugged the soft cotton fabric over her waist and down her legs.

"Mmmm," I moaned as I swiped my tongue through Jordyn's folds. She matched my moans with her own as her hips rose and fell, matching the strokes of my tongue.

"Ungh. That feels so good. Yes, baby, right there. Right fucking there." Her noises were pushing me over the edge. I used one arm to steady her, and I rolled onto my side to unbuckle my jeans so I could wrap my hand around my shaft and ease the ache she was causing. In the last seven months, I haven't been able to keep my hands, mouth, and other appendages off her. Jordyn was always irresistible, but pregnant Jordyn was like an obsession. She was as sexy and intelligent as ever, but she was carrying our child. She was a walking, talking miracle, and she was mine. "I'm close, baby. Hurry."

"How do you want me?" Pregnancy sex was intense and amazing, but our number of comfortable positions was severely limited.

"On your back. Help me get this fucking thing off." She sat up and began tugging at the dress. I slid it over her head and tossed it into the corner of the closet. She pulled off my shoes and took my pants off with lightning speed. I reclined onto my back and helped her straddle me. With her palms pressed into my chest, she slowly lowered herself onto me and began to roll her hips back and forth.

I covered her breasts with palms, testing their weight and marveling at how much they've grown in the past few months.

"Enjoying yourself?" She paused and eyed me quizzically.

"Always," I smirked and ran the pad of my fingertip down the dark brown line that ran down the middle of her belly, "You're so beautiful, Jordyn."

She answered me by digging her fingernails into my chest and throwing her head back. Her pussy clenched and spasmed around my dick, sending me over the edge. I gripped her thighs and thrust upwards, chasing her orgasm with my own climax.

"Whoa," she panted and grinned at me. "I really needed that."

"I think I'm developing my own closet fetish." I put a palm on her belly and splayed my fingers as I softened inside her.

"I would lean down and kiss you right now, but I can't reach." She chuckled.

"Hold on." I repositioned our bodies, so we were lying on our side and pressed our lips together. "Better?"

"Much better." She nodded.

"So, what are we going to do about this wedding?"

"I'll be fine. I just freaked out a little." She gave me a less genuine version of the smile I fell in love with.

"Baby, we don't have to go through with it. My parents got married in Vegas a week after they met, remember?" I wrapped her in my hoodie and hugged her close. It killed me to see Jordyn the slightest bit upset. I worried that planning a wedding while she was pregnant might be too much, but she insisted on getting married before the baby came.

"They were smart." She sighed and snuggled into my chest.

"Jordyn, I could text your doctor for the okay and have us on a flight in an hour. I just wanna be your husband. Most importantly, I want you to be happy, and I want you and our baby healthy... I don't give a shit about anything else."

"Mike, there are over four hundred guests coming." She picked up her head and narrowed her eyes, her mouth curling in a mischievous smile.

I shrugged and planted a kiss on her nose.

"You're serious?" She tucked her bottom lip in between her teeth. She was seriously considering my offer.

I nodded and planted another kiss on her nose.

"Okay." Her face spread into a wide grin. "Let's do it."

BONUS EPILOGUE: VEGAS, BABY!
PART II: JORDYN

"HOW ARE YOU FEELING, BABE?" Mike asked.

"Amazing," I said in a sigh.

I was flat on my back wearing a soft cotton terry cloth robe, a stark contrast to the tight and itchy layers of silk, tulle, and lace I'd been wearing when Mike found me. We were relaxing in the middle of an even softer king-sized bed with my fiancé massaging cocoa butter lotion into my feet. The smell was making me crave chocolate. After a one hour flight, room service, a shower, and sex in the shower, we were relaxing in the giant loft Mike reserved for us at The MGM Grand.

"I still wish you would have let me bring my laptop." I poked him in the chest with my toes.

"Nope. No work on this trip, my love." He kissed the bottom of the foot he was cradling. "When you wanna get hitched?"

I'd almost forgotten why we were here.

"Do we have to go right this second?" I'd never admit this out loud, but Mike whisking me away from work, and the wedding gave me my first real moments of peace in months. He always knew what I needed even if I was too stubborn to tell him I needed it. It was incredibly frustrating, and one of the millions of reasons I couldn't wait to wake up tomorrow as Jordyn Grayson. I also worried about telling Mom and Dad about our elopement. They were really looking forward to the wedding.

"No, I could stay like this for a while." He brought my foot to his lips again before crawling next to me on the bed and folding me in his arms.

"I've never been to Vegas before. I thought it would be bigger," I said. Mike's laugh vibrated against my back. "It kind of reminds me of Times Square. So bright and commercial." I wrinkled my nose.

"That's a fair assessment, but it's definitely bigger than Times Square. So, what do you want to do?" He kissed my nose, making me relax.

"What are my options?"

"We could take a nap. Have dinner. Go for a walk. Look at all the pretty lights. Gamble. Scope out a chapel…" He undid the sash on my robe and slipped his hand inside, running his fingertips along my bare waist, making me shiver.

"All of the above, please." I kissed him and moved his hand to my belly, where our baby was kicking up a storm. "Starting with the nap."

"Allow me to tuck you in." He opened my robe all the way and began planting kisses on my breasts and belly, making his way south. A moan escaped my lips when he found his intended destination, and within fifteen minutes, I was fast asleep.

———

"MIKE?" I peeked at him over my dessert menu.

"Yeah?" He raised an eyebrow at me.

"Why do you keep looking at your watch?" I eyed him from across the table at the ridiculously fancy restaurant he brought us to for dinner.

"What?" He glanced at his watch again.

"You have been glancing at your watch and checking your phone every few minutes."

"I didn't realize you noticed." He gave me a sheepish expression. "Work stuff."

"No work stuff on this trip, remember?" I raised an eyebrow.

"You're right. No work stuff." He reached for my hand. "So, in two hours, we're doing this?"

"Yup." I nodded and gripped his hand.

While I was sleeping, Mike preregistered us for a marriage license. Together, we decided to get married at the same chapel his parents got married in thirty-five years ago. Our reservation was at eight o'clock…in less than two hours.

"Are you having second thoughts?"

"About marrying you? Never." I smiled at him.

"Good." He brushed his lips over my knuckles. "Because I can't wait to marry you, and the deposit on the chapel is non-refundable."

"Well, now I definitely can't change my mind."

"Afraid not." He grinned at me. "You ready for some cake?"

"I thought the cake came after the wedding."

"I think we've already established that we're playing by our own rules, but if you don't want any, I guess that means more for me." He held his menu up and began to scour it, ignoring my glare.

"Well, I'm fine, but the baby wants the chocolate cake." I pulled his menu down and gave him a stern look.

"Oh, the *baby* wants the cake." He laughed.

"Yup."

"Well, we can't disappoint the baby."

"No, we can't."

Mike signaled for our server.

————

"THIS IS IT, BABY DOLL." We stood outside of the chapel. Mike had our marriage license in the pocket of his jacket, and he was gently squeezing my hand.

"Yeah," I said in a soft voice.

"What's up?" he asked with a note of concern.

"Nothing. I want to do this…" I tried to decide how to phrase my next thought because I didn't want to disappoint Mike after all of the effort he put into today. I didn't have to worry because he read my mind as usual.

"You wish your parents were here, don't you?"

That's precisely what was bothering me. The idea of running off with Mike and getting married in a little Vegas chapel was fun and romantic, but my parents have been by my side for every significant milestone in my life. As their only child, I could imagine how disappointed Mom and Dad would be when Mike and I told them we got married without them there to see it. What about Mike's family?

I nodded.

He took both my hands and pressed our foreheads together.

"Let's go inside and register. We can change our minds any time we want…and you probably have to pee again, don't you?"

I chuckled and nodded again.

"I love you, Micah Grayson," I said as he led me into the chapel.

"You better, Jordyn Robbins. I just dropped seventy-seven bucks on a marriage license."

"Goofball."

———

I WASHED my hands in the chapel's restroom and pulled out my phone. I was sure I wanted to go through with the wedding, but I would have felt better if I could get my parent's blessing. I took a deep breath hit send. The phone rang three times and went to voicemail. I was just about to leave a message when I heard a knock on the door.

"Babe, you okay in there?" Mike's voice called through the thin wooden door. I quickly ended the call.

"I'm fine. Coming out now." I stepped into the hallway to find Mike smiling at me.

"I thought I'd check on you." He brushed my cheek with the back of his fingertips. "The last time you said you had to go to the bathroom, you ditched my family and locked yourself in a closet."

"That happened a long time ago."

"Baby, that happened this morning."

"Did it?" I furrowed my brow and smirked. He nodded and kissed me. "How long until the ceremony starts?"

"We still have a few minutes. Why?"

"Do we have time for a quickie commemorating our last time having sex as single people?"

"I love the way you think, but I don't think we have that much time."

"Boo." I stuck out my bottom lip, and Mike bopped it with his finger. "Okay, handsome. Let's go get married."

We filled out the paperwork, signed the registry, and waited to be ushered into the main chapel.

"You kids ready?" The officiant greeted us holding a small bible.

Mike stood and helped me to my feet. She glanced at my bump.

"Congratulations. Do you know what you're having?" she asked.

"Hopefully, a baby," I answered with a smirk. Mike and I had no interest in learning the sex of our baby before they were born.

"Boy or Girl?" she persisted, not taking the hint.

"Maybe." I shrugged. Mike stifled a chuckle and squeezed my waist.

"Waiting to be surprised, huh? That's nice." She nodded before letting out a sigh. "Do you have a witness? If not, I can have the receptionist step in."

"I think we got it covered." He shot me a bemused look and waggled his eyebrows.

"What? Is Steve in there?" I laughed.

"Maybe," he said with a sly smile and kissed me before the chapel doors opened.

––––––––––

"MIKE." My voice was a breathy whisper as I tried to speak around a giant lump that formed in my throat. My parents were in the chapel, along with Mike's parents and Erica. For some reason, my dad and

Mike's dad were wearing matching Hawaiian shirts. I didn't have a chance to question it before Mom rush forward.

"Hey, pumpkin." My mother had tears in her eyes, but she was smiling. Her hands immediately went to my belly. "You are getting so big."

"What are you doing here?" I croaked.

"Well, we were planning on flying out in a couple days anyway. So, when Mike called us this morning, we changed our plans."

"Hey, baby girl." My father stepped forward and wrapped his arms around me. "You think I'd miss the opportunity to walk my favorite daughter down the aisle." He smiled, and I shook my head. My eyes were filled with tears of relief.

"I'm your only daughter," I choked out in a tear-filled laugh while the three of us held each other.

The comforting weight of Mike's hand was on my shoulder, and I disengaged myself from my parents, turning to face him.

"You ready, gorgeous?" He smiled at me. I mouthed the words, *thank you*, and he kissed my forehead.

"You look beautiful, Jordyn." Mike's mother cupped my face in her palms and used her thumbs to wipe away my tears. The simple white shift dress I wore was a far cry from the bespoke designer gown her son peeled me out of this morning.

"Maria, I'm so sorry about the dress fitting. I shouldn't have— "

"Tsk, tsk, tsk... Don't you dare apologize, sweetheart. Stress isn't good for my grandchild." She patted my belly. "And I can tell you from experience that this is one of the best places in the world to get married."

"It worked for us." Patrick put his arm around Maria's shoulder and kissed the side of her head. "Thirty-five years and counting…"

"Well, this is all lovely, but since I'm the maid of honor, it's my responsibility to fix the bride's makeup, so she doesn't look like a blubbering mess in her wedding photos." Erica pulled me aside, dabbed at my face with tissues, and touched up my face.

Within a half-hour, Mike and I were husband and wife. We celebrated with another dinner and, of course, more cake—at the baby's insistence. Erica left us to meet up with friends. Mom and Maria went to see Gladys Knight perform while Dad and Patrick hit the casino floor. Those two had apparently spent the hours before our wedding becoming best friends, which explained the shirts.

———

MY HUSBAND CARRIED me over the threshold of our penthouse suite and set me down on my feet in front of the bed.

"This dress is a lot easier to take off than the other one." He remarked as he pulled it over my head and tossed it over his shoulder.

"I'm glad you approve." I helped him out of his jacket and shirt. "Now, sit." I pointed to the edge of the bed. He obeyed. Slowly and carefully, I lowered myself to my knees and crawled between his legs.

"Thank you, Mr. Grayson." I planted a kiss on his chiseled abdomen and opened the zipper of his pants.

"You already thanked me for the beignets." He let out a low hiss as I began to stroke his length.

A throaty laugh tore itself from my chest. I lowered my mouth to the thick crown of my husband's cock and peppered it with gentle licks and kisses.

"Thank you for this amazing day," I whispered before sucking the flared tip into my mouth.

"You're welcome, Mrs. Grayson," he groaned and laid his palm on the back of my head, encouraging deeper strokes.

"Mrs. Grayson." I released him from my mouth and looked up to meet his gaze. "I like the sound of that."

"Me too," he groaned as I resumed pleasuring my husband with my mouth while he moaned and swore before finally exploding into my mouth.

He pulled me into his arms, and cuddled me in the middle of the bed.

"So, what are we going to do about the giant wedding in Calabasas?" I asked.

"We could still go through with it. Call it a vow renewal. An excuse to have a big party." He yawned before sliding his hand between my legs and lazily massaging my most sensitive spot.

"That's a great idea." I sighed. "I know my aunt Cookie was really looking forward to coming to California." I moaned contentedly as Mike quickened his strokes. "Her and Mom have been talking about it in my Instagram comments all week."

"So, it's settled." He held me in his arms after he'd brought me to climax. "I'll take any excuse to marry you again." He sucked my arousal off of his fingertips, winked at me, and flashed me a sexy, filthy grin.

I grabbed his face and kissed him again, trying to convey all of the emotions that I had no words for. Eighteen months ago, Micah Grayson found a stranger in a new city, desperate for adventure while browsing in a bookstore, and turned her life into a fairytale. My heart was so full of love for the man holding me in his arms that it felt like it might burst.

"What was that for?" He laughed. "I'm not complaining. I just want to know so I can do it again."

"You are such a goofball, Mr. Grayson."

"Is that a good thing, Mrs. Grayson?"

"I don't know. Let's see how the next thirty-five years go."

. . .

THE END

Usually, this is the point in my one of my books where you would find the Spotify playlist containing songs featured in and inspired by the book.

(If you're interested in my book playlists you can find them here. I worked really hard to put them together and I think they're pretty good.)

Instead here's a list of all the books referenced in the story. I have personally read and enjoyed all of these books. Mike & I both cut our romance teeth on Jude Deveraux's Velvet Quartet — tag yourself: I'm definitely an Alyx— and Brenda Jackson's annual reunion cruises are definitely author goals.

Most of the books on this list are small press or indie published and all of them can be purchased at The Ripped Bodice:

1. The Duchess Deal - Tessa Dare
2. The Princess Trap - Talia Hibbert
3. The Bromance Book Club - Lyssa Kay Adams

4. Velvet Promise, Velvet Song, Highland Velvet, Velvet Angel by Jude Deveraux
5. Indigo - Beverly Jenkins
6. Forget Me Not - Brenda Jackson
7. White Whiskey Bargain - Jodie Slaughter
8. Pink Slip - Katrina Jackson
9. Everything She Never Wanted - Tasha L. Harrison
10. A Duke by Default - Alyssa Cole
11. Rafe: A Buff Male Nanny - Rebekah Weatherspoon
12. Daddy - Jack Harbon
13. Cherishing the Goddess - Lucy Eden

*NOTE: DADDY BY JACK HARBON IS NOT CURRENTLY AVAILABLE FROM THE RIPPED BODICE, BUT I NEEDED THE TITLE TO MAKE THE JOKE WORK—I HOPE IT WORKED. HOWEVER, KITTEN BY JACK HARBON IS SOLD AT TRB AND IS ALSO A VERY GOOD BOOK.

AUTHOR'S NOTE

Dearest Reader,

Thank you for reading Blind Date with a Book
Boyfriend.

The idea for this story hit me after my last meeting
with the incredible romance authors of the
RWANYC chapter. I was naturally excited about my
upcoming signing and wanted to do something to
commemorate the event.

The Ripped Bodice has fueled some major mile-
stones in my short writing career. I decided to make
the leap into self-publishing after reading The 2016
State of Romance in Publishing Diversity Report.
Almost a year later, I'd published my first paperback

and The Ripped Bodice was the first store to carry Everything's Better with Kimberly on its shelves. A signing at TRB is on every romance author's bucket list and I'm still pinching myself.

Ordinarily, one would buy a souvenir coffee mug & take a selfie in front of the store. I decided to write a book.

I hope you loved reading Mike & Jordyn's story as much as I loved writing it.

For those who asked and anyone who may be wondering, if by some chance I get invited to do another signing at TRB, I will write Erica's story.

PS If you loved Mike & Jordyn's story & want to share the love via social media, here's a link to some promo images you can use: bit.ly/BDWABBPROMO

Don't forget to tag me: @lucyedenauthor on face-book, instagram & twitter, because I'm nosy.

THANK YOU:

To Zaida Polanco, thank you for accepting my ridiculous phone call, only saying that it was bad idea once and telling me everything fun and romantic about Culver City while I scribbled down your every word. I'm so glad you're pleased with the finish product. If it flops, I'm blaming you.

For the record, I still think the Sinner joke killed. Get it? Killed? Okay, I'll see my self out.

The T&T crew. Thank you for inspiring me to improve simply by being better at writing than I am & thank you for talking me out of writing things that are sure to get me canceled.

My amazing beta readers Marina Garcia, Lydia San Andres & Lory aka "Fact or Fiction" Wendy who read every word of this story, practically as I was writing and helped me eliminate all the eye rolling and the monsters.

Kai for editing this story with almost no notice. You're a rockstar.

Romance Rehab, especially Jennifer, for your brilliant author services, particularly, the blurb critiques. You will pleased to know that Mike now longer bites his bottom.

Judy, thank you for catching all of the words I missed and deleting all the extra spaces.

My ARC team for giving their time and energy to read my work and help spread the word.

Thank you so much, dear reader, for reading Blind Date with a Book Boyfriend!

I hope you liked it. Please consider leaving a review wherever you share your good news!

February 2020

xoxo,
lucy

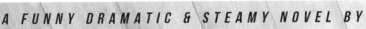

LUCY EDEN

EVERYTHING'S

better

WITH LISA

2-6-5-3. Red X.

"Fuck!"

2-6-5-3. Red X.

"Shit!"

I typed my code into the keypad a third time with no success.

"Goddammit!" I kicked the wood doorframe of the hundred-year-old Harlem brownstone I'd called home for the past six years.

"Hey, asshole! Shut the fuck up!" a female voice shouted from the ground-level apartment.

I looked over the banister to see a short woman with waist-length, chestnut-colored hair staring up at me, holding a baseball bat.

"Crystal?" It was too dark to see her clearly. I was definitely more than a little buzzed, and my biological mother was the only short woman with long dark brown hair I knew. But why was she holding a baseball bat, and why was her voice different?

With a little difficulty, I walked down the stairs to get a closer look. The woman took a step back as I approached and held the bat higher, tightening her grip on the neck.

"My name is not Crystal, and I live here."

Upon closer inspection—as close as I could get without getting clocked in the head, anyway—I could tell she definitely wasn't Crystal. She was younger, way more beautiful, with pale golden brown skin and she didn't have my birth mother's bright blue eyes. Crystal also moved back to Missouri four years ago. Most importantly, tiny Babe Ruth definitely didn't live in my house. I was drunk, but not that drunk.

"You live in here?" That wasn't exactly how I meant to phrase that, but my brain and my mouth weren't cooperating. Also, I'd become aware that I was leaning against the brick wall of the stoop to support my weight.

"Yes," gorgeous, not-Crystal hissed. "I live here." She was so sincere that I was hit with a wave of confusion, and when it ebbed, realization slapped me in the face. I took a step back and looked up at the door I had been kicking a moment ago, then I looked to the right at the door I should've been kicking.

"Shit." I did it again. I went to the wrong fucking house.

Why did these brownstones all look the same?

I turned to head to the brownstone where my code would work, and I guess I turned too fast because I stumbled and had to grab the railing to keep from crashing to the ground.

"Are you okay?" She lowered her bat, but she didn't take a step forward. I was drunk. I tried to enter the wrong house, and almost busted my ass in front of my sexy neighbor.

"I'm fine, *Crystal*. Mind your business." This ordeal was embarrassing enough without Batgirl, suddenly concerned for my welfare.

Hadn't she just called me an asshole?

I didn't need her help. I was a grown-ass man who needed to walk twenty feet to his front door.

"Excuse me?" she said. "Again, dickhead, my name is not Crystal, and you screaming in the middle of the night woke me up from my much-needed sleep, so it is my business."

I turned to face her and felt myself sway as I tried to stabilize. Her outburst was sexy as fuck and I felt an overwhelming urge to kiss her.

Nope. Nope.

That was definitely the alcohol talking.

I can't kiss her.

I have to get home.

The word *home* floated to my consciousness, but instead of focusing on that goal, I decided to speak.

"You kind of look like my mother, but not really. Her name is Crystal. I'm fine. Just got confused. My house looks exactly like my sister's house." I pointed at the brownstone next door before pointing at Kimmy's.

"Your sister?" She gave me the look, the skeptical look I get when people found out about my adopted family. One would think I'd gotten used to it after all these years. Maybe it was all the tequila shots, but tonight it pissed me off. She continued, "The woman that owns this brownstone is not your sister, and I'm not your mother, so you need to take your drunk ass home, to your actual house, before I call the cops."

"Kimbery Shimmins is my shishter!" I yelled as I backed away from her towards my house. I could hear myself slurring my words and considered the possibility that trying to walk and talk at the same time wasn't the best idea. I turned toward my house, continuing to amble forward. "And I'm glad you're not my mom because my mom is awesome, and you'd be a shitty mom with your baseball bat and your potty mouth."

Even though I was sure I just used the words "potty mouth," I knew I'd said something profound because I was met with silence.

I turned to look at her and found her expression blank. A loud and expletive-filled response was what I expected, but she just stood there, frozen and a little sad. A feeling like regret crept over me, but I couldn't figure out what I should have felt regretful about. I tried to replay the last thing I said, but I couldn't fucking remember, something about Kimberly and a shitty potty?

That look... I couldn't stand seeing it, so I turned away from her and climbed the steps to my door, where I typed in the four-digit code.

Green checkmark.

———

THE THROBBING in my head woke me up before I could open my eyes. I'd stayed out late drinking last night and stumbled into bed fully clothed. Again. I barely remembered anything after Beck Cameron's last round of shots. I must have taken a cab home, and I vaguely remembered meeting someone last night. A woman—a beautiful woman who was pissed at me for some reason. I climbed out of bed and trudged to the bathroom, swallowed two Advil, and turned on the shower.

The hot water beat me into consciousness, and memories of last night began to float together in tiny little patches. I had tried to get into Kimberly's house last night, thinking it was mine. We used to have the codes to each other's houses until I went to her home by accident one night, and her fiancé almost beat the shit out of me with a hammer before he realized who I was. Apparently, the nickname Thor had more significance than his resemblance to Chris Hemsworth. The thought ignited a flicker of a memory. The beautiful woman I met last night had a baseball bat. She was outside of Kimberly's house. I said something to upset her, but I couldn't remember what it was. I focused on putting myself together and getting to work.

———

AFTER A STOP AT STARBUCKS, I stepped off of the elevator at seven forty-five. Technically the offices didn't open until eight thirty, and unless we were working on a big case, the senior associates and partners usually didn't show up until after nine. I was a first-year associate, which meant I always had to be here, working my ass off, but not busy, in case one of the partners needed something. My father was also a partner at this law firm before he became a judge, so I also had to prove that I wasn't just a rich kid using Daddy's connections. My dream had always been to work for Hollander and Cameron ever since my dad would bring me here as a kid. I wanted to be just like him. Whenever Crystal was in trouble, we would come to this building, and her lawyer, Reginald Simmons, would fix everything like a superhero. He was also a legend at the firm and was now a United States district court judge, so I'm sure my presence at the firm wasn't purely based on merit. That's why I was determined to work twice as hard as everyone else.

"Good Morning, Judy." I flashed the office manager a grin and handed her a venti mocha latte, 130 degrees.

"Thank you, Cole." She snatched the cup from me and took a sip. "There is not enough coffee in the world. Did I ever tell you how much I love you?"

"Every day, but I never get tired of hearing it," I called over my shoulder. I sat at my desk, or a fancy version of a cubicle, and started working.

In the years I spent daydreaming about being an attorney, I thought it would be closer to *Law and Order* and not hours sorting through discovery requests, filing motions, and reading depositions for hours. It would be worth it if the work were fulfilling. I wanted to become a lawyer to help people like Crystal and me. Most of what we did at Hollander and Cameron involved helping rich people get richer.

Discovery requests in the movies usually depicted someone running into a conference room carrying a file that held the one piece of paper that was the key to winning the "big case." In reality, discovery requests could be four boxes of documents that need to be combed through carefully to find a specific piece of information that may or may not be there. This was a task for first-years. Most of my morning was spent sifting through three years of email conversations from a real estate company looking for any mention of steel beams.

"There he is," Beck Cameron called behind me. He was the son of Bryce Cameron, one of the managing partners. He'd have a good shot at following in his father's footsteps if he wasn't such a fuckup. Beck's voice was still raspy from last night. "How the fuck do you do it?"

I turned to face him. He was in the same suit he wore to work yesterday, a pair of sunglasses, and sipped something green out of a giant clear Starbucks cup.

"You look like shit."

"I feel like shit." He dropped into his chair.

"Are those the clothes you had on yesterday, man?" They smelled like last night too.

"Well, I didn't exactly make it home yesterday." He dropped his sunglasses and raised his eyebrows. "If you know what I mean…"

"You mean, you met someone at the bar last night and went to their house to have sex," I deadpanned.

His expression soured. "Maybe if you tried it once in a while, you'd be in a better mood."

"I'll think about it." I turned back to my computer.

I ignored Beck and tried to focus on work, but the only thing I could think about was my bat-wielding neighbor.

———

IT WAS a quarter to nine when I finally stepped off of the subway to make the five-minute walk to my house. My parents lived in the brownstone on the corner. I saw that the front parlor light was on, and my stomach had the Pavlovian response it usually did whenever I got in proximity to my mom's kitchen. The growling also reminded me that I worked straight through lunch and skipped dinner.

Walking into my parents' house was a crapshoot. Mom and Dad were always affectionate growing up, but since the three of us moved out... Well, it was always a good idea to announce yourself when you came in.

"Mom? Dad?" I yelled after taking off my shoes and walking into the empty sitting room.

"We're in here, baby," Mom called. It sounded like she was in the dining room.

The faint melody of Marvin Gaye's "What's Going On" played as I found my parents sitting on opposite sides of the table wearing their reading glasses and hunched over laptops, probably working on real estate stuff. Dad was a judge, and Mom was a psychiatrist, but together, they had invested in real estate around New York since the early nineties, and most of their money came from those properties. It was how their three kids were able to afford their own brownstones on the same street.

"Are you just getting home from work?" Mom asked as I kissed her on the cheek. I nodded and loosened my tie. "That's ridiculous." She wrapped one of her deep brown hands around my chin and tipped my head to the side as if she were inspecting me for damage. "Look at this luggage under your eyes. Are you getting enough sleep?"

"Beverly, leave that boy alone." Dad closed his laptop, removed his glasses, and pinched the bridge of his nose, squinting.

"They are working him too hard. Look at his face." She still gripped my chin and forced me to look at my dad.

"Please. My easiest day as a public defender was worse than my hardest day at HC, and I had lives depending on me. He'll be fine." Then he narrowed his dark eyes at me and muttered, "He'd be better if he stopped staying out late after work and took his butt home at a decent hour."

It was time for me to make my exit.

"Where was all this sympathy when I worked all those late hours?" he asked.

"You are not my child, and if memory serves me correctly, and it always does, I took care of you plenty..." She released me and eyed my father suggestively.

"You still do," he replied in a voice too deep for my comfort.

It was really time for me to make my exit.

I cleared my throat to remind them I was still in the room. Mom laughed and patted my face.

"Go in the kitchen and fix yourself a plate. Kimmy is in there, so you better hurry if you want some corn."

I swung the kitchen door open to find my sister scooping the last of the corn out of a large bowl and dividing it between two plates. She was a younger version of my mom with chestnut colored skin and long dark tightly coiled hair which she'd pulled up in a bun. She wore a sleeveless blouse and yellow pencil skirt so I guessed she came here straight from work too.

"Hey, Stringbean." I took the bowl from her and managed to salvage some of the corn. The salty, buttery smell made my stomach growl again. "You opening a soup kitchen?"

"No," she said and tried to snatch the bowl back before I held it out of her reach. "Adam's working late, and I'm making him a plate."

Adam was Kimberly's fiancé. They'd only been together for a few months, but he was a good guy and made her happy.

"I thought he was moving to Barbados." I clutched the bowl while I reached for a plate.

"He is, but he had some meetings in New York, and Vittoria can't fly anymore. So, we're both in the same place at the same time for a few days." Her face spread in a wistful grin and she started scooping baked mac and cheese onto the plates.

My sister was the executive assistant to the head of the real estate and hospitality division of Wolfe Industries, a Fortune 50 company. Usually, she was jet-setting around the world, but her boss was in the latter part of her pregnancy and couldn't fly, so she was home more often. Adam was an architect and was building a luxury resort in Barbados for Wolfe. He flew back and forth a lot and was preparing to move there for the foreseeable future. Long-distance relationships were supposed to be hard, but these two seemed to make it work. I wasn't a fan of long relationships, much less long-distance ones.

My sister and I managed to divide the leftover meatloaf and cornbread without coming to blows, though she took all four corner pieces. We were wrapping our plates in foil when I remembered last night's encounter.

"Hey, do you have a tenant?"

She froze. "Yeah," she answered in a slow, cautious tone. "Why?" She turned to face me, eyeing me with suspicion.

"How long has she lived there?"

"She moved in about eight months ago. Again, why?"

"She's lived there for eight months, and I've never seen her?"

"No." She shook her head and went back to covering her plates.

"No, what?" I asked, knowing exactly what she meant and tried to stifle a grin.

"Stay away from her. She's sweet. She minds her own business, and she always pays her rent on time."

"Excuse me? Your sweet tenant who minds her own business tried to attack me with a baseball bat last night."

She whipped around to face me.

"What? That doesn't sound like—" She almost said her name, then stopped herself. "Why did she try to attack you with a bat?"

"I might have accidentally tried to get into the wrong house last night." I shrugged and reached for the cake dish.

"Again, Cole?" She glared at me and dug her fist into her hip.

"*Yes, Kimberly*," I mimicked her. "You know all of the houses look the same at night."

"And when you're drunk?" She tilted her head and raised her eyebrows.

"I am a social drinker. I work ten-hour, high-stress days, then I have a few drinks with some of the other associates after work. It's networking. It's an important part of my job."

She narrowed her eyes and pursed her lips, mimicking Mom's *you're so full of shit* face. "You really need to get your shit together, Cole." She turned and started slicing into the yellow cake with chocolate frosting.

"You know what, Kimmy? You're the last one who should be lecturing me about facing hard truths."

"And what the hell is that supposed to mean?" She turned to face me, but she held the knife.

"Put the knife down, and I'll tell you."

She looked down at her hand, snorted a laugh, and dropped the knife on the counter.

"Where are you taking those plates?"

Her smile dissolved, and she hesitated before answering me, not meeting my eye. "To Adam's apartment. So…"

"When's the last time he stayed at your place?"

"We're not in court, Cole. Could you get to the point?"

"He's still acting weird about the brownstone and the fact that you have more money than he does."

"You're ridiculous. It's none of your business, and Adam is just more comfortable at his place. I love his apartment, and I love him, and we're hardly in the same place long enough for it to become an issue. And now that that's settled, let me reiterate that I want you to leave my tenant alone. She's been through a lot, and she's not your type."

"What do you mean she's been through a lot?"

"Again, none of your business." She'd finished piling and packing her plates and slid them into one of the five hundred plastic shopping bags Mom kept in the cabinet under the sink.

"And what do you mean she's not my type? What the hell is my type?"

"The type of woman who steals your sister's jewelry when you invite her over for family dinner…"

"That happened once."

"Or the type of woman that proclaims at a family barbecue that she didn't know Black families could adopt white children."

"That was a different chick, and in my defense, she seemed a lot smarter when I met her."

"Bye, Cole." She walked to the kitchen door. "Leave my tenant alone and fix your life."

"Love you too, sis!" I yelled at her retreating form.

She stopped, sighed, and turned to me.

"I'm sorry for all the shit I just said. You're amazing, Fruity Pebbles, but you have horrible taste in women, and your current life choices are questionable."

"You really suck at apologizing. You know that?" I cracked a smile, and she chuckled. "So, I'm amazing but still not good enough for your sweet, bat-wielding tenant?"

She heaved a sigh. "Look, I'm not at liberty to share her personal business, but I don't think it's a good idea."

"For her or for me?"

"For either one of you."

———

THANK you for reading this bonus chapter of Everything's Better with Lisa. For purchase information please visit geni.us/EBWL

AN ANGEL FOR DADDY
NOVELLA

RUBY HAYES IS INTELLIGENT, beautiful, great at her job and loves her students. She's not too fond of me because despite moving to this small coastal California town only a month ago, I've managed to get on her bad side by consistently arriving late to pick up my daughter, Nina. It's probably for the best. Between my job and adjusting to raising a little girl by myself, adding romance to the equation isn't something I have time for.

Spencer Jones is successful, handsome, a doting father and terrible at reading a clock. His daughter, Nina also happens to be my favorite student. Getting involved with the parent of a student is bad idea, no matter how witty and charming they might be. It's probably for the best. Between my job, taking care of my dad and climbing out debt, a new relationship is the last thing I need.

SPENCER AND RUBY have plenty of reasons to stay apart, but can a little divine intervention and an assist from a pint-sized cupid teach them a lesson that will last a lifetime?

———

FOR PURCHASE INFORMATION *please visit* geni.us/AAFD

RESOLUTIONS

NOVELLA

MIKE IS MY BEST FRIEND.

My tall, gorgeous, and bearded best friend.

We both share a love for music, Monty Python, dirty jokes and my grandmother's homemade cookies.

I also have a giant crush on Mike.

And he has no idea.

I tried to tell him at a New Year's Eve party last year, but I lost my nerve, and he ended up with someone else.

Armed with a broken heart and a massive hangover, I wrote a list of New Year's resolutions intent on turning myself into New and Improved Jane who doesn't let life pass her by.

With resolutions to check off the list and limited time to finish, I accepted Mike's offer to help.

But spending all this time with Mike is bringing up feelings that I'd spent a better part of a year keeping under control. Mike has a girlfriend and I can't risk losing my best friend, but sometimes the way he looks at me makes me think, maybe, he feels them too?

I'm probably just daydreaming, as usual…

This novella has NO cheating and is a standalone, friends-to-lovers romantic comedy full of alphas, steam, sarcasm and Monty Python references

———

FOR PURCHASE INFORMATION *please visit* geni.us/LERES

BEAR WITH ME

NOVELLA

Hi, I'm Celestine Woods, most people call me Chellie. If you are one of my 850K followers, you might know me as the super successful Instagram influencer, but more than likely you probably know me as the woman who got dumped by her former rockstar boyfriend, who then publicly professed his love for his new girlfriend in a song on Spotify before getting engaged a week later.

. . .

WHILE I THINK I had a perfectly rational response to this news, my sponsors didn't agree. Apparently no one wants to buy expensive skin cream from the woman who had an alcohol-fueled meltdown at the biggest New Year's Eve party in the world.

Now, I'm at Black Bear Mountain Lodges, a cabin resort in the Catskill Mountains, to relax, recharge, and rehab my image... and toss in a couple of sponsored posts, 'cause a girls gotta eat. The only hitch in my plan for R&R is the sexy, yet grumpy, lumberjack who runs the resort. His people skills leave a lot to be desired and it's no wonder that I'm the only guest at this place.

I know nothing about living in the mountains and he knows nothing about marketing and publicity. His resort and my image could both use a little TLC, so we formed a truce and teamed up to help each other.

Between my social media know-how, my smartphone, a gorgeous grumpy mountain man and a strangely friendly bear that keeps coming to my window every night, we can get this all turned around... right?

Who's ready for project #ChellieInTheWoods?

A disgraced Instagram influencer uses a mountain retreat in an attempt to rehab her image with the help of a grumpy lumberjack, who is more than he appears to be.

This novelette has NO cheating and is a standalone, contemporary shifter romantic comedy full of alphas, steam, and sarcasm.

———

For purchase information please visit geni.us/BearWithMe

ABOUT THE AUTHOR

Lucy Eden is the *nom de plume* of a romance obsessed author who writes the kind of romance she loves to read. She's a sucker for alphas with a soft gooey center, over the top romantic gestures, strong & smart MCs, humor, love at first sight (or pretty damn close), happily ever afters & of course, steamy love scenes.

When Lucy isn't writing, she's busy reading—or listening to—every book she can get her hands on—romance or otherwise.

She lives in New York with her husband, two children, a turtle & a Yorkshire Terrier.